Inkblots
and Blood Spots

STORIES AND POEMS BY
MICHAEL BAILEY

FEATURING THE ILLUSTRATIONS OF
DANIELE SERRA

"Most writers are either stylists or story-tellers. The stylists tend to be more common in literary fiction, the storytellers more common in genre work. Michael Bailey's prose is highly accessible, but very precise … he's a stylist, his prose very clean. Michael is indeed a very literate storyteller. His stories are always darkly sharp-edged in tone, texture, and delivery, easily appropriate for genre fiction. But perhaps most important, his stories are about something … each one is built on a meaningful, engaging, intellectual premise. I highly recommend this short story collection, which includes some compelling and delightful poetry."

– Gene O'Neill, author of *The Cal Wild Chronicles*

"Artfully executed. A unique and powerful contribution to speculative literature."

– Tim Deal, *Shroud Quarterly*

"Between e-books, Amazon, and new presses springing up seemingly overnight these days, a reader can easily end up with choice overload. Luckily, fans of both traditional horror and the more subtle, complex terrors of the psychological kind need look no further than Michael Bailey's *Inkblots and Blood Spots*. His short story and poetry collection is a cornucopia of dark, diverse treasures: richly detailed historical fiction like "The Dying Gaul," a re-imagining of characters from Lord Byron's poem *Childe Harold's Pilgrimage*; psychological thrillers like "A Light in the Closet," in which a little girl receives a most unusual, yet perhaps not entirely unexpected, nocturnal visitor; classic Gothic chillers like "I Wanted Black," about one man's harrowing reckoning with the past; genre-defying stories like the *Fahrenheit 451*-inspired "Fireman / Primal Tongue" and the sci-fi / horror nightmare "Bootstrap;" as well as more traditional sleep-with-the-lights-on stories like "The Mascot" and "Not the Child." With *Inkblots and Blood Spots*, Michael Bailey delivers the kind of startlingly original, beautifully imagined, and deeply affecting stories that linger long in the mind, and even longer in the psyche."

– B.E. Scully, author of *Verland: The Transformation*

"This collection of captivating stories and poems is both haunting and poignant. Filled with love and loss, the weight of these resolutions echoes out into the darkness with a heartbreaking permanence."

– Richard Thomas, author of *Disintegration*

"Michael Bailey continues to amaze. He is on track to becoming his generation's Ray Bradbury."

– F. Paul Wilson

For those who guide me down this ever-darkening path
with literary brilliance:

Gary A. Braunbeck
Mort Castle
Neil Gaiman
Brian Keene
Stephen King
Dallas Mayr
David Mitchell
Thomas F. Monteleone
David Morrell
Chuck Palahniuk
F. Paul Wilson
Douglas E. Winter

Inkblots
and Blood Spots

Stories

Poems

Introduction

When the fiction of dark fantasy and horror defaults, whether through commerce or complacency, into the lock-step of genre, new voices emerge, typically in short stories, to rage against the defining and confining walls. Think Ramsey Campbell, Dennis Etchison, Clive Barker, David J. Schow, Thomas Ligotti, Joe Hill. Now add Michael Bailey to that list. *Inkblots and Blood Spots* is ambitious, inventive, in love with language, and a joy to these jaded eyes. Bailey turns plots, characters, expectations, and even words inside out with courageous abandon. His desire to tell different kinds of stories (and to evoke complex emotions—sorrow, loss, melancholy, awe—as well as dark fiction's more familiar shock and dread) is relentless. This is not a collection to miss, but one that I suspect will be long-remembered.

– Douglas E. Winter
November 2014
Reykjavik, Iceland

Beneath Clouds

The rain
hammers down
burning the skin
heavy and viscous
melting away
the layers
of ache
and
the ice
slices through
cutting the breath
with significance
chipping away
the slivers
of hope

the snow
gently falls
casing the life
gray amid ashes
covering up
the layers
of time
when
the sun
used to shine
warming the heart
without consequence
melting away
the layers
of love

Hiatus

The light turned from red to green but that didn't seem to get things moving. A woman in the car ahead of them absentmindedly faced the empty road with her hands at ten and two, no longer the proper way to place them on the steering wheel, according to his daughter. Haley was only twelve and forever lecturing Seth on his driving habits. One of Haley's favorite songs had been playing on the stereo. Haley sang along with Bono from U2 and they crooned: *Have you come here for forgiveness? Have you come to raise the dead?* And then Haley stopped singing.

Seth waited a few seconds before trying the horn.

Come on, lady.

No one was behind them, or at any part of the intersection for that matter. It was just the two vehicles on the road: his Prelude and the immobile Pontiac Extinct, as he liked to call it. One of her many bumper stickers made him snicker: TIME DRAWS NIGH. Another read repent or die. She was waiting for the end of the world. The great silence—

That's all there was, Seth realized. Silence.

The back of his fist hitting plastic was the only sound that emanated from the horn, and there was no music from the stereo, no slow sputter of engine. Everything was silent.

It was all so strange.

Haley sat next to him in the cabin, legs crossed. She held her feet and peered out the windshield, her mouth open. She looked tranquil, stuck on a note, not singing.

The light green.

Haley, he said.

Everything around him was stopped on red.

Haley, he said louder.

He pushed against her shoulder in a panic and she moved; like a rag doll, her body crumpled against the passenger door.

Haley!

Seth laid her across the seat while checking her still pulse while his own raced. She was dead.

Eyes glossy, his daughter gazed at the ceiling.

Haley, come back to me, goddamn you!

He slapped her cheek. CPR proved difficult upside-down, so Seth went around to the passenger door and let himself in. Was it three breaths and five compressions? Five breaths and ten compressions? Oh god. It always looked so easy on television. A few breaths and she'd be back to normal. After tilting her head back, he put his mouth to hers and watched her chest rise and then slowly fall, put his ear to her lips—nothing—and tried again. One breath. Two breaths … did it really matter?

Don't you do this to me.

Leaning over her body, he felt for her sternum and started the compressions and counted one and two and three and four and—

Come on!

He continued with a single hand—pushing down

hard but not too hard—while he dug in his pocket for the cellular. His phone worked to a certain extent: the buttons depressed, a battery icon showed three-quarters full, the signal good.

dialing … it read.

He couldn't remember dialing emergency. It was all a blur. He put it on speakerphone and returned his full attention to Haley. He breathed into her a few times and checked for a pulse.

To the phone: Why aren't you dialing?

To his daughter: Come on, baby.

Nothing. A lifeless doll.

She was so small; his fingers wrapped around her wrist and then some.

dialing …

The stereo displayed the time, as well as the channel they were listening to before everything turned silent. Both the stereo and his phone told him it was 8:08, and all he could think about was that they were late. Eight minutes late for school and they still had a few miles to go. Not that it mattered now. You can't teach the dead.

Breathe for me, baby girl.

He tried to hang up and dial again, but the phone was frozen, forever dialing. Seth frantically pushed every button to no avail. The dots weren't blinking; a solid dot dot dot after the lying word and nothing more. The phone was as useless as the car.

The Extinct ahead of them hadn't moved.

The light green.

The woman facing the road.

Hold on, Haley.

He brushed her cheek with the back of his hand.

I'll be right back, love.

Seth ran to the passenger door of the other car and banged on the window.

Hey! I need your help. My daughter, she's not breathing.

She remained facing the road, hands at ten and two.

Hey!

He ran to the driver's side door and found the window down. The woman looked ahead aimlessly. She wore silver hoops in her ears with dangling quarter-carat diamonds. Caroline had a similar pair. A gift he had given her for their anniversary. If only she were here.

Please, lady.

Seth tapped her arm.

No response.

Look, I want five damn seconds of your time. My daughter—He grabbed her shoulder and shook her. She admired the road, ignoring him. Pushing her shoulder, she teetered; not stiff, but as lifeless as a mannequin. Her car was just as silent, the stereo on and the tachometer showing a steady idle, yet soundless and inert. Seth waved a hand in front of her face before pressing his fingers to her neck. She was dead, too.

Somebody help!

No traffic or distant horns, no construction noise, no wind. His lifeless daughter waited for him.

Seth returned to his Prelude.

How do you restart a car that's already on? No sound came from turning the key, forcing the accelerator to the floorboard did nothing; the switches for the lights didn't work, nor did the windshield wipers, windows, or locks.

He tried them all. Cursing, he pounded his fists against the dashboard until they were numb.

Seth slid Haley across the seat and scooped her up and continued yelling for help as he carried her away from the road and onto the sidewalk. There was a man walking out of the drugstore on the corner of Main Street and Canterbury, but he wasn't really walking anywhere. The man's legs were parted in mid-step, the glass door ajar with a cockeyed OPEN sign hanging from the door handle. He was nothing but a statue holding the door for a stationary man at his back. Seth walked by and wanted to touch him, to see if he was real, to see if either person were real—but his hands were demanding Haley.

Farther down the sidewalk was a woman in a paisley dress frozen with her English bulldog. The leash between them was taut and the dog's tongue hung from its mouth like a chewed piece of bubblegum, saliva dangling from the tip. Mid-stride, both of them. The woman held a cell phone to her ear and when Seth was at her side he freed a hand, took it from her, and kept walking. She didn't seem to mind.

The display told him she had been talking to Mom.

Hello?

Mom wouldn't answer.

He tried the buttons, but of course they were useless. The digital clock on the screen read 8:08, like the others. The phone broke apart when he dropped it, the phone and battery and battery cover flying in three different directions the moment it smacked against the concrete. He didn't mean to drop it, but it slipped out and fell and there was nothing he could do. At least it was sound, something to hear besides his quickening footsteps.

When did you get so heavy, Haley? You've grown so fast.

About three blocks down, Seth came across a Toyota Tacoma in the road following a beat-up minivan of no discernible make. The pickup was tailgating, but they weren't moving, so what did it matter? He peered inside each as he passed. Same story, as if they had been speeding along the road and had abruptly stopped. By the time he reached the end of Main Street, Seth had walked close to a mile, his body covered in sweat, his face streaked with tears. He couldn't remember the last time he had cried aloud; but here he was, sobbing like a child as he held his dead daughter draped over his arms. Haley's eyes were beautiful and open and looking to heaven. He thought of closing them, yet couldn't bring himself to do it. She was as close to alive as he could have her and he wanted to keep her that way. He had to get home to Caroline. To see if she was dead like the rest of the world. A desire burned inside to bring his family back together.

There were a dozen vehicles paused on the road and he had passed another half dozen of the standing dead. Another mile and he was home, legs sore, muscles aching. Every person he passed along the way he had expected to come alive again, reaching for Haley, wanting to take her away from him, wanting to close her eyes for good.

Two miles was an easy walk; carrying the dead weight of your twelve-year-old daughter for two miles was something entirely different.

He made it home and crumpled to his knees on the front porch, taking Haley down with him. He laid her to rest on the porch swing, her arms and legs curled in a fetal position, eyes wide and looking right at him.

I'm not ready to sleep, Daddy.

Seth had only imagined those words.

Her sweet voice, so innocent.

You don't have to sleep, baby. You can stay up as long as you like. Daddy needs to rest here a while. He's tired, but he loves you.

His attempts to knock on the door were pathetic.

Caroline?

Louder knocks.

Caroline?

Is she sleeping too, Daddy?

I sure hope not, Haley. Wait here while I go see. It took most of his effort to rise and he used the doorknob to help haul his body from the ground. The door was locked, but that was normal. After letting himself in with the key, he called for Caroline a third time.

It was her day off, a day to herself. She should be home.

Honey?

From the doorway, he could see that both the kitchen and living room were empty. The door to the bathroom in the hall was cracked open, but lights were off throughout the house. Open shades let in enough sun so that no lights were needed during the day, and Caroline was a stickler for not using electricity unless absolutely necessary. She was probably home.

He peeked around the corner to see Haley curled on the porch swing. He couldn't leave her, not while he searched the house. It wouldn't feel right. Instead, he brought her inside and set her on the sofa and propped one of the couch pillows under her head so she'd be more comfortable. Why he did this, he didn't know.

Love you, Daddy.

I love you too, baby.

He kissed her forehead and checked the other rooms, calling for Caroline. There was an open bottle of Chardonnay on the dining room table, but no wine glasses set out for her or any of her friends had they come over.

He checked the backyard: empty.

Garage: empty.

The only sign of Caroline was an unfinished load of laundry in the dryer. The cycle was stopped with ten minutes left on the timer. Seth opened the dryer to find clothes still damp. He closed the door, tried the button—nothing. And then he saw the telephone and ran to it.

No dial tone.

Of course not.

Caroline was waiting for him, he knew. He'd find her on the bed, toes up, leaning against a pillow with a dog-eared novel in hand. *In Silent Graves*, by Gary Braunbeck, or *Mr. Hands*, perhaps. Those were a couple of her favorites. He'd find her staring vacantly at the pages. But she wasn't on the bed, nor was she in the adjacent den. He knew where she was hiding because the door to it was closed—the master bathroom. She always closed the door when taking a bath. It was one of those odd things she did, like crinkling her nose after saying something snide, or snorting at the end of a laugh and continuing to laugh because of it. He knocked and called her name before letting himself in.

Placid water surrounded her body from the neck down. A dry knee was raised above the bathwater to help prop the paperback, but Caroline was no longer capable of reading the pages. She was dead. He stood there a moment, hoping that she'd place a finger against the current page and then look over her reading glasses, smiling.

She had died peacefully, at least, like Haley.

He kneeled next to her and took the book, marked her place out of habit with a new dog-ear, and set the book aside so he could take her hands. She held them out to Seth, fingertips touching fingertips to form an upside-down heart, as if she were expressing her love to Seth one last time. He kissed the heart as a single tear fell from his cheek and into the water, creating rivulets on the surface. The bathwater was warm, almost hot. She couldn't have died long ago. 8:08, he guessed. She sometimes stayed until the water cooled. Invisible marionette strings held Caroline's pose when he pulled away. Seth grabbed her chin gently and tilted her head so she faced him. Her eyes were incredibly beautiful.

I'm sorry, love. Whatever this is, whatever happened …

Seth sat with her a while before lifting her out. He held her wet body in his lap and rocked, the water dripping around him, soaking into his clothes. He dried her off with a towel and carried her to bed. He dressed her, held her, brushed a hand through her hair.

If only he could have his wife and daughter back so he could say goodbye.

The last thing he had ever said to Caroline was a pathetic attempt at flattery, something trivial about the drawstrings of her pajamas coming untied and how he wanted to untie them further.

If only he had said I love you. And Haley. Feet off the dashboard, he had said. The last things he had ever said to his family before his jaunt to the paranormal.

I love you, Caroline.

He wiped his eyes and attempted a smile, but couldn't find one anywhere.

I love you back, Seth, she'd say.

How long have I been lying here?

Apparently, it didn't matter. The alarm clock on the nightstand revealed a familiar time. Somehow he knew if he unplugged it from the wall, the time would stay there, like the light in the bathroom when he had tried turning it off by the switch. However the world was the moment all of this happened, forever it would remain. Seth thought of the clouds hovering in the sky, airplanes and whether or not they'd fall, waves in the ocean, the weather in general. What about places in the world where it was raining, or snowing? What would that be like? The sun—would it set, or continue baking the earth? What about the animals, the billions of people?

I'm the only one.

You're not alone, said Caroline, her lips unmoving. It's what she would have said if she were still alive. *You have us.*

You're right. I have you and Haley.

And Sally, Haley would add.

In Haley's room there was a small, black metal cage lined with hay and fitted with a water bottle and feeder. Sally was Haley's white bunny, small enough to fit in her hands. Sally was a boy, but Haley had insisted on calling him that. Sally—it's long for Sal, she had informed him. And then she told him that his own name wasn't long or short for anything. You have a boring name, Daddy, she had said. Seth knew the bunny would be dead too, but he'd check anyway. He brought Haley into the room and laid her next to Caroline. They looked so alike, the two of them. They gave him the same empty gape, pleading with their glossy eyes for him to stay as he stood in the doorway.

I'll be right back.

Sally's head was by the feeder. He had been eating when he died. Seth opened the cage door and took the bunny by the scruff of his neck. His body was still warm, and it was then Seth realized that his wife and daughter were the same. Soft and warm. He petted Sally behind the ears and along the back. Dead, yet so alive.

Like a veterinarian, he inspected the animal by holding it up to the light of the desk lamp. A pellet of food was lodged in his mouth, his pink button nose crinkled like Caroline's. Two small marbles for eyes. God knows why, he touched one of them, not knowing what to expect. What he got from it was a feeling of revulsion, like he had poked a bunny in the eye and nothing more. A sick part of Seth wanted to throw the animal as hard as he could at the wall.

He started to squeeze.

Daddy?

Seth spun on his heels and dropped the bunny—a soft thud against the carpet.

Haley wasn't there.

Sal's okay, baby.

After putting him in the cage, Seth returned to the bedroom. See? he told his family. I wanted Sally to be in here with us. He's family, too.

He set the cage at Haley's feet and joined them on the bed. He ran his fingers across her forehead and through her hair. He held Caroline's hand, closed his eyes.

We're going to wake up from this bad dream, I promise.

He woke a few times throughout his sleep, peering between clenched eyelids at his unmoving family. He tested for a reaction in Caroline's hand each time, hoping she'd squeeze back, but her hand was always limp. The window across the room revealed a sun that hadn't moved, the same suspended clouds, the same finch perched on the window-sill with its wings partially outstretched. Eventually, he shut the blinds so he wouldn't have to be reminded that the world was on hiatus. He later covered the window with a blanket when he could no longer put up with the light. After it continued flaunting 8:08 in glowing red on the nightstand, he unplugged the power cord of the alarm clock. Seth wanted to sleep, mostly in hopes of waking up from this nightmare; but he was unable to do even that.

Not with his wife and daughter in limbo, their bodies forever warm next to him.

On the third day of madness—guessing at time, by this point—Seth dug the graves.

The weather was right for it: the sky stuck on early morning, the air cool yet windless, the ground unbelievably soft and wet from a downpour the night prior to Seth driving his daughter to school. It seemed so long ago. According to the world around him, however, it was no time at all. It was the very next second, maybe not even that.

He was hesitant on digging only the two graves, but what point was there if he decided on ending his life prematurely afterward? It's not like he could cover himself in dirt to be in the ground next to his family. He didn't bother digging them deep, either. What point was there? Their bodies wouldn't rot; they'd remain perfect indefinitely, and there weren't any live animals around to dig them out, which was the whole point of digging graves so deeply in the first place. He started with Caroline's and then dug one for Haley. The holes were each about two feet deep and just long and wide enough to hold their bodies. Seth listened intently the entire time for sounds other than that of his shovel. For anything.

But there was nothing.

He was alone.

It took everything he had to carry Caroline and Haley to their plots in the backyard. He had checked the clocks in the house one final time. They revealed that time was irrelevant. The only reason for time is so everything doesn't happen at once. Einstein said something like that. What the hell did he know?

Is it time for bed, Daddy?

Yes, baby. It's time for bed.

He set her body into the smaller grave and kissed her brow.

Time to sleep, he told her while closing her eyes.

Come to bed, Caroline would say, were she able to speak.

Seth placed her into the ground and closed her eyes as well. He kissed her on the lips; they were soft and moist and for a moment Seth thought she had kissed him back, the air in her lungs finding way into his mouth somehow; but he had only leaned against her body, forcing the reaction. She still tasted like strawberry lip gloss.

It took as long to settle on covering them with dirt than it did to unearth the dirt from their graves.

He kneeled in front of them, crying for hours or for no time at all. He held a clump of dirt in each hand—one for Caroline and one for Haley—but he could not bring himself to do it. Their eyes were closed, but Seth knew they were still alive behind their lids, watching him, pleading for him to stop.

He covered the bodies with white bed sheets from the linen closet. It was the only way he could bring himself to toss those first handfuls of dirt onto them—a sound he'd never forget. Amidst the silence, the sound of dirt pattering against the sheets was riotous; the more he added, the less noise it made and the easier it became. He stood and lobbed shovelfuls over their bodies, and then used the shovel to push the rest of it over them.

Soon he was left with level ground and masses of dirt next to the graves roughly the size of his wife and daughter. He piled that on as well, and then threw the shovel across the yard where it smacked against the fence.

Seth collapsed, his body covered in a mess of sweat and earth, hands blistered and burning and clenched as tightly as he could manage.

What about Sally?

He had forgotten Sally at the edge of the bed. He had meant to bury the bunny with Haley.

It's time for bed, baby. Time to sleep.

But what about Sally, Daddy?

I'll take care of him.

And what about you?

I'll take care of me, too.

A burned-in image of Caroline in the tub turned him away from taking a shower. But cold water would be so refreshing, and the dirt he covered his family with plastered his body like brown war paint, reminding him of death. And the smell—that earthy decay mixed with perspiration—it was everywhere. The water wouldn't run, he knew; it would remain trapped in the pipes *ad infinitum*. Was there a Latin phrase for turning the giant hourglass of time back over again? Probably. Was that what had happened? All the sands of existence spent, the last granule fallen? Who cares?

No one. They're all dead.

A stranger said those words; a dirty reflection of a worn man, the last man whose heart still ticked at the end of time. This dirty man wiped away some of the filth with a washcloth doused with water from a bottle someone had left on the kitchen counter. Seth was behind there somewhere.

He already knew how he was going to do it, how he was going to end his life. It was all planned out during the timeless hours he'd spent digging the graves.

He had to go into town first.

He took the Schwinn and brought Sally with him. He knew riding down the street on Caroline's pink bicycle was a strange thing to do, especially with a bunny nestled in the wicker basket attached to the handlebar. He would have taken *his* bike, but the wheels were flat—he apparently hadn't ridden it for a while—and holding Sally would have proven difficult. What did anyone care? He couldn't take the car because the engine wouldn't turn. It wouldn't even try. It had given up like everything else in the world.

Seth wasn't even sure why he had taken the bunny until he was halfway into the city. Sally carried his sanity.

Thousands of people, frozen in place. Sally gave him the smidgen of comfort he needed while weaving in and out of motionless traffic, along the sidewalks around pedestrians, wherever was easiest to ride. He felt their eyes trying to connect to his; whether walking or behind the wheel, Seth felt them watching.

They were all watching.

Seth knew Walmart sold guns and had them readily available. He passed through a petrified parking lot filled with cars playing Tetris and silent people holding awkward poses: filling trunks with plastic bags, returning shopping carts to designated areas, a man in a wife-beater finagling his cart onto a curb, an obese woman riding a motorized cart, a pregnant teenager with an arm sleeve of tattoos holding her belly with one hand while a child half her age tugged the other, a bald man scratching his ass, a homeless man holding a cardboard sign.

The last grains of sand.

Seth leaned the Schwinn against a woman exiting the glass doors and went inside.

The store greeter refused to greet Seth, but he didn't mind a crazy man bringing an animal into the store, either. No rush of people. No overhead music. Only mannequins masquerading as customers. Seth avoided their eyes by counting tiles on the floor. The hunting section was on the opposite side of the building. He only bumped into one person on his way to the guns, a young woman dressed in scrubs who was reaching for some kind of boxed toy high up on a shelf. He apologized out of habit as she fell over and crumpled to the floor. He kept walking.

No one was there to help him at the counter, so he

helped himself after finding the clerk with the key to the gun case. He chose the most expensive shotgun, which he assumed would be the most reliable, and loaded it right there on the counter with a single shell. It was all he would need.

Sally sat on the glass.

What?

The bunny stared at him innocently, nose in mid-crinkle. If all of this is really happening, then nothing matters anymore. I could splatter you across the counter.

Seth switched off the safety and pointed the 12-gauge at the creature. Pressed his finger against the trigger. Hesitated. He hadn't considered whether or not the gun would work. It was a mechanical device. Did that matter?

Sally's dead. It doesn't matter if I shoot him.

He looked around the store at the various customers.

It doesn't matter if I shoot any of these people.

He squeezed the trigger tighter and at the last moment decided to redirect the barrel. The shot was deafening and took out a light fixture hanging from the ceiling. Shards of florescent bulb rained over him.

The gun nearly flew out of his hands. Part of him hadn't expected the thing to work. A comforting drone from the blast replaced the silence. All at once he realized he could take his own life and be with his family. He could never be buried with them, but he could join them in death. Suicide and populicide, all rolled into one. He remembered the word from college. It meant 'the killing of all people.' Seth was all people now, he supposed … the last man alive.

Sally under his arm, he headed outside into the stale air. The bike was there waiting for him, leaning against the woman at the door. He nestled Sally in the basket and managed the shotgun over the handlebars. It was an inelegant ride, but soon he was passing cars on Main Street.

Traffic thinned ahead and he found himself pulling up to the Pontiac Extinct with the TIME DRAWS NIGH bumper sticker. It was stopped at the traffic light where all this had started, his vacant Prelude behind it. He rolled up next to the woman and smiled, remembering how he had frantically pounded on her window, how he had raced around to tap her arm to ask for help after trying to revive Haley. The woman facing the road. Hands at ten and two.

She turned to him and smiled.

Seth fell over the bike as he tried to back away. He crashed hard within a metal mesh of handle and foot pedal and chain that pinned him to the street. Sally, dazed, hopped out of the wicker basket, his nose crinkling as he chewed the pellet of food still in his mouth, his left eye winking spastically. Seth set off the shotgun and sound rushed in all at once: tires squealing, glass shattering, people on the sidewalk screaming, his car idling, cell phone dialing in his pocket. The no longer smiling woman now sped away with a panicked expression. The man walking out of the drugstore collapsed and searched for the missing part of his thigh, the door behind him red. The young woman in the paisley dress tried to run away, a barking English bulldog anchoring her to the sidewalk. Seth admired white battleship clouds floating gracefully through a blue sky. And then he thought of Caroline and Haley buried in the backyard, their hands clawing at dirt.

Seth wrestled the bicycle free and snatched Sally by his neck, then hurried into the car and slammed the door. Still open as he sped away, the passenger door banged shut as he rounded the corner on Main Street and Canterbury. Sally somehow managed to stay on the seat as Bono crooned about crawling and holding on when all you got is hurt.

The clock on the stereo changed to 8:09 when he heard the phone in his pocket begin dialing. Had he placed the call prior to Haley falling against the door? He looked to the empty seat next to him as he fished in his pocket.

Caroline! I was calling Caroline.

The display read *dialing* … the dots blinking this time.

Come on, love, pick up.

Seth knew she couldn't answer and imagined Caroline—she always carried her cell—with her pocket ringing, the sound muffled by the almost two feet of dirt covering her body; Haley next to her, screaming against the packed ground covering her mouth; the world around them black and airless.

He gave up on the phone, his mind questioning the graves. Would there be enough air in the soil to last until he got home if they couldn't dig themselves out? Had he packed the ground lightly? Densely? Were their chests too compressed by the weight of the dirt to even try?

The clock on the stereo read 8:12 when he pulled into the driveway. The car was still rolling when he jumped out of it, Sally riding shotgun. Calling their names, Seth ran around the side of the house and into the backyard.

The ground was level, except for Caroline's fingers clawing the air like earthworms escaping the rain.

Barely moving and cold.

Time may have ceased for a few days unchanged, but her body had been buried in the wet ground long enough for it to cool her down a few degrees. Seth grabbed her hand and tugged. Her hand squeezed back, desperately, her nails cutting into his skin. Unburied, she collapsed over Haley's grave.

Seth rolled her out of the way and kept digging.

Alive

Can't you see
the mud?
I taste it, choking
Hands hold me down
my hands reach out
to hands
not holding me down

Can't you see
the weight?
I feel it, crushing
Hands hold me down
my hands reach out
to hands
not holding me down

The sweet air / my lungs are still breathing
The warmth / my heart is still beating
The crushing cold / I taste it
The cold / I fucking hate it

Can't you see
I am alive?
Can't you see
my hands reaching out?

Bootstrap /
The Binds of Lasolastica

Virtual partition 242 not responding
Adjust array parameters …

Partition 242 had periodically failed over the last few weeks during initial testing on Bill Chevsky, and Victor knew it was finally time to migrate the data elsewhere.

He had the 500 terabyte partition waiting in the cloud. It would be simple to replace because soft drives were physically non-existent, at least from his vantage point, yet the process was cumbersome. Storing bio-drives in-house was impractical and too costly; it was much more cost-effective to rent the space at an offsite facility, which he had visited prior to starting the project. As Victor replaced the faulty partition for Bill, he wondered how much of the human mind he was replacing and how much knowledge a single partition contained. It didn't quite work that way, however, because each was useless without the others. The 241 other partitions were figurative puzzle pieces of the Chevsky array, and it would take many more. How large was the mind of man? That was the penultimate question; the ultimate was whether or not cloning could be done on the mind.

The last test Victor ran on Bill had filled twelve peta-bytes of data, or twelve thousand terabytes. The transfer was close to completion, or so the system reported before it had crashed. The fifty-strand, wide optical catheter cable at Bill's neck was warm from the gigabits upon gigabits of ones and zeros passing through it per second.

Thirteen years prior, a young student at MIT and his peers created a company called ImagEnation, commonly known as the company responsible for founding the Artificial Knowledge Project. Victor had attended the Nobel Prize ceremony in Nepal and could still picture the kid holding up his palmtop computer to the audience. "This device," he had said, "contains the Webster's dictionary, the English language in its entirety," a break for audience applause, "and the complete history of the American People. This is the future of technology. This is the future of education. This is the future of the model U.S. citizen." The screen behind him showed a woman of Mexican descent on a hospital bed with wires connecting to various places on her head, from which acupuncture-like needles protruded. This spider web of wires coupled with a thicker set of cable plugged directly into a similar palmtop computer. When the next slide appeared, Victor laughed. With all the advanced technology in the world, they were still using slideshows for presentations. The next slide displayed numbers and parabola charts. The next slide showed the crowd a progress bar and the next a woman getting 'disconnected' from the contraption. The last was a picture of the same woman holding a miniature U.S. flag in one hand and citizenship papers in the other. ImagEnation had programmed a woman to be more American than most Americans.

**Virtual partition 242 not responding.
Adjust array parameters …**

While moving Bill's data, Victor thought of the woman and how a part of her psyche had been replaced as easily as swapping a virtual partition … a Mexican programmed as an American, thanks to the Artificial Knowledge Project. They had brought her onstage after the slideshow and she gave a speech in perfect Americanized English, without a hint of Spanish accent. She gave her testimony on how it had changed her life for the better.

Want to be a helicopter pilot? Victor asked himself as he established the new partition. "Why not," he said aloud when it initialized. *Trigonometry, calculus, advanced theoretical mathematics?* All it took was a little programming, and money. But such things were singular applications. Victor wanted the whole shebang, an operating system, the vessel capable of running programs. Sure, some punk kid from Delaware found a way to store the knowledge and language of the American People onto a compressed 200 gigabytes, but no one before had pushed the limits of the human mind. No one had ever attempted to store the entirety of a well-educated mind onto digital storage.

The facility hosting the storage space provided three six-foot tall racks with the capacity to hold 512 bio drives, and enough power to supply twenty watts to each. This was just the storage, a small part of a larger storage cloud, which replicated to various other data farms around the world for backup and recovery purposes. A fourth rack held the server farmstead, an even dozen mega computers, as they were often called, connected and clustered as one. The front display of racks was clean and black and filled with blinking blue and green lights, a beautiful spectacle; the back of the rack was a massive plethora of multi-colored optical and power cables. A generator connected to the multi-AC controlled room, a device capable of providing enough redundant clean power to the building for outage scenarios. The project also required a sizable amount of money. Through a company generically labeled HVS, Human Vitalogy Systems, Victor was able to fund close to two billion dollars in private short-term investments. He figured the money would last about a year.

Array status healthy

The display screen reported good news for once. The replacement partition was live and slowly absorbing into the array. It would take about an hour before it would be ready to accept data. Without disconnecting Bill from the programming station, Victor gently woke him. He was merely asleep. All it took was the turn of a knob and the drugs feeding into his wrists did the rest.

"Bill," he said, and waited for eyes to focus.

"Victor?"

"Did you rest well?"

"Yes. I could sleep for days. Did it work this time?"

Victor sighed, put a hand onto Bill's shoulder and said, "Almost. Listen, one of the virtual partitions went kaput and I had to suspend data copy in order to replace it. You're still connected, so I can't let you up yet."

The restraints were only a precaution. He didn't want Bill to wake up on his own accord and accidentally roll off the bed. That would be bad.

"I was wondering if you wouldn't mind going a second round. Shouldn't take more than three or four hours."

"What time is it?"

"Two in the morning."

"Monday?"

"Yes, Monday."

"I could use the sleep."

Victor smiled, turned another knob, which shot a dose of Pentithazine through the length of a second catheter, and watched Bill's eyes roll under their lids. In a matter of seconds, his project had returned to R.E.M. sleep.

He met Bill Chevsky a few years back while visiting his mother in the hospital. Both Bill and Victor's mother had been diagnosed with Lasolastica, one of the incurable cancers, which had adapted over the years to the common medicines used to treat other cancers like Leukemia, Melanoma, and Lymphoma. Laso took your life in less than a few months in most cases, and it quickly took his mother's. Bill wasn't far behind. Victor could already see cheekbones through Bill's semi-transparent skin, the dark shadows under his eyes and the fear of death hidden behind them.

When his mother died, Victor pledged to find a way around the cancer, a way to cheat the incurable disease. It was simple, really, logistically; the process was the complicated part. After the second Gulf War, the United Nations—or Untied Nations, as Victor liked to call them—declared an unwinnable war against human cloning, similar to how the war on terror was handled decades before. But his method of fighting was legal according to the Cloning Laws.

There were five main stipulations of the Cloning Laws,

known on the streets as *The Five Cloning Commandments*:

> *1. A license issued by the Department of Human Modification is required to clone body parts of any nature;*

> *2. Cloned animal body parts, not of human nature, may be used to serve either humans or animals requiring medical attention, if such parts are adaptable;*

> *3. Cloned human body parts may be used to serve either humans or animals requiring medical attention, if such parts are adaptable;*

> *4. Body parts of any nature may never be cloned for monetary gain; and*

> *5. The human central nervous system, thus including the brain, spinal cord and cranial nerves (retinas excluded), may not be cloned under any circumstances.*

There were many other facets to the laws, but those were the five basic principles. The Hippocratic Oath was even adapted.

Victor's idea was to clone an entire human body except for the central nervous system—to keep his experiment entirely legal—and then reprogram the original, which would later be transplanted into the cloned healthy version of the diseased or dying body. Sven Morrigan from Norrköping, Sweden had attempted such a feat a few years prior—minus the reprogramming—but the patient mind did not properly adapt and the patient was pronounced brain-dead shortly after her body was reanimated. Further studies revealed that the patient's brain had hard-reset, its internal memory and storage wiped clean, in other words. The doctor had rebooted the body, as well as the brain, but the brain was as useful upon reanimation as a reformatted drive, or a bunt cake, for that matter.

Continue with data copy? (y/n)

"Yes, please."

Victor pressed y and leaned back in his chair, thinking of cake.

The copy of Bill Chevsky was at 78%.

He watched the display for the next few hours, adding partitions when needed. Twelve thousand petabytes were used by the time the image reached 87%, an amount of storage he had reached on his last experiment with Bill, and this included compression. What bothered Victor was that he had reached 91% by this mark on his last run. Had Bill changed that significantly in only a week, enough to warrant such an enormous amount of storage difference? Could possible data corruption be to blame ... aka brain damage? Perhaps bad sectors on drives were similar to damaged neurons within the brain. The thought of defragmenting the human mind sent shivers up his spine because it was highly possible and worth looking into with future research. He made a note of it, realizing he could quite possibly be cloning damaged sections of Bill.

Victor had read articles comparing neuron storage within the brain to the physical storage of bio drives, and they were remarkably similar in nature. "The storage capacity of the human brain is infinite and cannot be set to a numerical storage value," proclaimed a Dr. Moresco from Syria. "Like the Universe, the brain is forever expanding." Years ago, a Dr. Birge from Syracuse University had placed such a numerical value upon it, stating that brain capacity ranged anywhere from one to a thousand terabytes, an amount that was quickly disproved. His initial guess was a dismal 3TB. While incorrectly hypothesizing the storage potential of proteins, the bio drive was born many years later because of his experimental research, using genetically engineered DNA to store data rather than magnetic or metallic medium. Intel had revolutionized the microprocessor not long before by replacing traditional transistors with controlled deoxyribonucleic acids. It was estimated during his time that the brain contained billions of neurons—somewhere between fifty and two hundred—and that each neuron interfaced with thousands upon thousands of other neurons through trillions or possibly quadrillions of synaptic junctions, with each synapse possessing a set numerical value. This equation produced an estimated half to full petabyte of potential data, which was also incorrect. Victor had disproved that theory while researching MLSP, or Molecular Level Storage Potential, while attending Berkley. His research followed the neuron / synaptic junction equation, but added to it exponentially when his findings proved that ones and zeros could actually be controlled on a molecular level.

Virtual partition 242 not responding
Adjust array parameters …

A long, drawn-out sigh replaced the silence. Bill's breathing wasn't much louder.

"242. Again," he told his unconscious patient. "What is with you and partition 242, huh?"

The display read 93%.

"We're almost there, Bill. We're going to do this."

While replacing the partition yet again, he thought of his mother, his reason for the insanity behind the need for this type of accomplishment. Like his mother, Bill's body was going to die. His mind, if that could be saved …

I could use the sleep, Bill had said to him.

His mother had said something similar just before passing. "I'm taking the long sleep," she had said. The longest sleep possible, one from which she'd never wake. Victor didn't want Bill's last words to be "I could use the sleep" because it was all too familiar.

Array status healthy
Continue with data copy? (y/n)

A sigh of relief.

"Yes, damn it. Yes."

Life, the waking dream.

94%.

She had looked similar to Bill while on her deathbed, with dark sunken eyes, pale gray and slightly transparent skin, blue spider web veins underneath feeding the cancer throughout her body. He remembered holding her fragile hand as she looked to him with distant eyes. Her skin, cold and clammy. She had looked past him, Victor knew, to the other side. She could see it and he knew by her expression that she was afraid of going there alone. Even with those last fighting breaths and her body pumped full of poison, she wanted to live; seeing that only made Victor want to die right there next to her so they could at least be together.

Data copy complete
Checking array for inconsistencies
Please wait …

"Do I have a choice?"
He had never gotten this far before.
"Cross your fingers, Bill."
Unconscious, Bill faced the ceiling. Victor crossed Bill's fingers for him. He had fallen asleep happy and was still smiling, anxious about possibly entering a disease-free copy of his body, living again, freed from the binds of Lasolastica.

Data corruption found in array
Correcting …
No errors found

"Well, which is it?"
As if answering him, the screen displayed:

Image creation successful
18,216,369,102,558,196

How large was the mind of man?
For Bill Chevsky, the answer was a little over 18.2 petabytes. Take that number and multiply it by eight, and that's

the number of ones and zeros used to portray Bill digitally. Hypothetically, Bill was the first human being with two minds, one physical and the other digital. One of his minds was virtually and quite literally in the clouds, a data storage cloud holding all 18.2PB of him. In terms of psychology, this sort of gave Bill a dissociative identity disorder.

Could it be done?

Could the human mind be cloned?

The answer was now yes, and Victor was the first to do it. He wanted so badly to wake Bill to tell him the good news, but if he did, he'd have to do it twice because he couldn't be disconnected from the catheter cable while conscious. It would most certainly kill him. Instead, he followed procedure and disconnected him properly from the computers and from the cloud that now hosted a copy of his mind. Victor turned the knob again to send wake-up juice into Bill's wrists, and he slowly opened his eyes. He yawned.

"So?"

Victor smiled.

Bill cloned it.

"Really?"

"We did it, Bill. You have a digital twin."

"When can we try?"

"Soon. I want to run thorough consistency and integrity checks on your image."

Bill smiled again. Looking at him was like looking at his mother the moment before she died—the eyes cloudy and distant, the smile full of effort and skeptical hope. He didn't say anything, but nodded.

"Tomorrow afternoon."

"Okay."

"You look puzzled."

"Oh … my mind is going through some loops. Questions, you know? I've been thinking about it for a while. There's technically two of me in the world, right? *Me*," he said, pointing to his chest, "and then me," he said, pointing and looking to the ceiling. "Another me is floating around out there in the data cloud, but I don't know him. I can't feel him. A part of me thinks I should be able to feel that connection somehow. Does that make sense? The version of me that's talking to you is going to die, but the other gets to live. But it's not *me*, is it? I mean, it *is* me, but not *me* me."

The same questions had been haunting Victor's mind.

"*This* body is going to die. I know that. I'm not going to be a part of it after tomorrow afternoon because my mind—with *my* actual brain—will be in my new body …"

"It's a shell, Bill. Your body, it's just a shell and nothing more."

"But you know what I'm getting at, right?"

"Look, what makes Bill Chevsky Bill Chevsky is in here." Victor pointed to his temple. "We've gone round and round about this in our preliminary consults. What we're doing is strange, no doubt, and it's never been done before, but we're taking a good mind from a bad body and we're putting it into a healthy, good body. A new shell. It will still be *you* in there."

"Can I see him?"

"Before the operation? Of course."

"I mean after."

"You want to see your old body? I'm not sure that would be a good idea, Bill."

"I want to see him."

"Bill …"

"Promise me, Victor. You owe me that much. If a cloned copy of my mind is going into a cloned copy of my body, I want to look into my eyes to know it's no longer me in my dead body, that what's left after the operation is just some … I don't know, some soulless, brainless husk and nothing more. I don't want a funeral or anyone to know. I want to see that diseased body cremated."

"Everything will be taken care of, I assure you. And please don't refer to your body as a husk. It makes this entire operation seem so Mary Shelley *Frankenstein*. We've come a long way with science since man—or woman. in this case—came up with the idea of reanimating life with a donor brain, some metal rods, and a lightning storm. This isn't science fiction. This is life. And your life in this body will end soon and start again in another. From today on, I mean. Everything up until the image was created will be transferred to the new body, of course."

"What does that make me?"

"What do you mean?"

"I mean right now. Right now doesn't matter much, does it?"

"I'm not following."

"This image, it encompasses everything about me, from the moment I was born until the moment you woke me a few minutes ago. Every thought, every learning experience and failure in my life and everything that makes me who I am today … that time span of my life is what is on that image. Not now. Now doesn't matter because now isn't on the image you're transferring to my new body. This conversation we're having about this very conundrum—it won't matter much tomorrow afternoon because it won't exist in Bill Chevsky version two. You'll remember it, but the new me never had this conversation. It isn't on the image. Get what I'm saying?"

"I do, Bill, but look—"

"So everything I do from here on is pointless," he said, tears welling around his eyes. "What does that make me?"

"It makes you—"

"Non-important, pointless—"

"It makes you unique, Bill. We've all dreamed as little boys, as adults even, to have a clone. To be at two places at once; one of us to stay home and take care of the chores while the other plays. Am I correct?"

Bill nodded. "That and to be invisible."

"Your situation is a little different, that's all. One of you gets to go out and play while the other, well, passes on."

"I want to look into his eyes tomorrow, Victor, to know that he's not me."

"Bill."

Bloodshot and tired eyes stared back. He was a man clinging to life, a man afraid of waking up from his operation and seeing more than his lifeless body. Perhaps a man who once believed in souls.

"I want to sleep tonight. I don't want to live any longer than I have to. In fact, I need you to put me under now. Anesthetize me, or dope me up somehow and let me sleep. The thought of a pointless existence will drive me insane otherwise. I want to dream the ultimate dream. I want to wake up tomorrow in my new body. I'm tired of this one. Will you do that for me?"

The last thing Victor said to Bill Chevksy version one:

"I will, and thank you."

He was thanking him for more than the opportunity of performing the procedure, what could quite possibly end up being the gateway to a new treatment for patients with terminal conditions; he was thanking Bill for his mother, and for sacrificing his body for the hope of mankind and for the next generation of medicine; for the twelve-year-old girl who will never see thirteen because of the tumor growing on her spine; for the single father who will never see his son graduate because of heart failure; for the newborn born into a life destined for Laso or any of the other incurable cancers.

They had started cloning the body prior to the trials. It was a heavy expense, but funding had already covered the body. It was waiting for them in what Victor liked to call "the shop," a facility in the adjacent building. If Bill was anything like Victor's mother, he didn't have long to live. The night, would it be forgiving? Apparently so. He had injected Bill with enough drugs to assist him into a coma, and the next morning Bill's numbers on the electrocardiograph revealed he had survived his final sleep.

Victor recorded the old body vitals and signaled the surgeon team. He watched from behind the operating room glass with a select few responsible for funding the project. Not one stayed for the gore, excusing themselves with "This is excellent work, Victor … most interesting, but I need to make a noon appointment …" or similar lines of encouragement to hide their weak stomachs. One by one they left him and soon he was alone, leaning forward in his seat, nose to the glass, eyes moving like a metronome: to and fro, to and fro, to and fro between the health monitors and his patient; the clock on the wall keeping tempo: tick tock, tick tock, tick tock for the next four hours.

The surgery was invasive, to say the least. An ungodly sight. The key was to keep Bill Chevsky alive during the ordeal, something of which Victor had no control over as he nervously awaited behind glass. The thought of Bill alive as they cut away and removed the skullcap and exposed the membrane—it chilled him; the thought of a man in a coma with eyes still able to see as they detached the retinas, removing most of his face to get to the hidden cranial nerves beneath, cutting away cheekbones, removing the lower jaw, nose and upper row of teeth until there was not much remaining of his head—it repulsed him. A set of surgeons removed pieces of Bill while others worked eagerly to keep the rest of his body alive, injecting medicines, stopping blood flow, suctioning blood spill and feeding new blood to replace that which was lost during the operation. Bill Chevsky, once a normal-looking man, was now a body hacked from the waist up, organs rerouted and placed onto trays out of the way, cables and clamps coming out of a chest peeled open like a banana with the fruit scooped out. They supported the brain before removing the rest of the skull, and then they cut away all remaining and unnecessary soft tissue—as well as bone matter—to expose the central nervous system whole: brain, spinal cord and cranial nerves. The workspace around them was remarkably clean throughout, despite the mess they had made of Bill's body. And then they unplugged him. Three sets of red-gloved hands lifted out the one thing Victor could not clone because of the fifth stipulation of the Cloning Laws: The human central nervous system, thus including the brain, spinal cord and cranial nerves (retinas excluded) … They took it out of him and gently placed it onto a stainless steel tray. Bill Chevksy version one was dead. All vitals on the electrocardiogram had flat-lined.

The lead surgeon looked over his mask to Victor and gestured a bloody thumbs-up. Nurses wheeled the massacred body out of the room—a brainless husk, Bill had said earlier. He was right. Victor would be there alongside him to destroy it. Arm-length rubber gloves were replaced on those staying for the second phase of the operation, and they held their arms to the ceiling as they waited for the clone. A doctor rinse-washed the brain and everything connected to it with bottles of clear liquid. She began placing electrical nodes onto it, which would send a minimal amount of current through the exposed central nervous system until transplanted. She finished as the new body was rolled in on a mobile operating table: Bill Chevsky version two.

It was nice to see him whole again.

While they were hacking apart Bill's old body, surgeons in an adjacent operating room had prepared the cloned body for transplantation. Their precision showed; a lack of anything to show would be a better way to phrase it. Only smooth lines were visible where they had made incisions, and they were only visible when the body was flipped onto its side. The entire back of the skull was removed, but would be completely hidden after the piece of bone was replaced and hair grew. Empty eye sockets let in light from the room, revealing that the cranium was empty. Everything else was intact from the face, from what Victor could see from his perspective. The large piece of skull lay next to the body. A straight cut extended from the middle of the back to the base of the skull as a means of entry for the central nervous system. Bill would have a generous scar after they sewed him back together again. Victor wondered about Bill's eyes, and then a nurse walked in with a small cooler, which held the cloned parts of Bill that needed to be installed after the brain, spinal cord and cranial nerves were placed into the body and reconnected. The entire process took them late into the afternoon.

After another thumbs-up, Victor prepared "the shop" for the reimaging process while he waited for the body. Surgery had come a long way in the last fifty years. It was remarkable he could work on him the same day. When they wheeled in Bill version two, it looked as though he were simply asleep on his back, chest rising and falling without the need of a nebulizer. New lungs with auto-inflation / deflation made sure he stayed breathing while an artificial heart kept synthetic blood pumping throughout his body. Various forms of nanotechnology were used to repair damaged tissue, and to keep the body in a controlled coma; to quash the coma, it would take only a small electromagnetic pulse to turn off the bots, thus forcing the body to take over.

"Thank you for bringing him to me alive."

"He's a vegetable," said the doctor pushing the gurney, "but a healthy one, at least. The rest is up to you. We all have our fingers crossed."

"We'll get you back," Victor said, patting Bill on the shoulder.

The electrocardiogram displayed a slightly higher than

normal heart rate, but blood pressure and pleuth were regular. Bill's image was finishing its final data integrity check while Victor readied the fifty-strand, wide optical catheter cable and injected Bill with another dose of Pentithazine. The last thing he needed was for the new body to wake up prematurely. Bill's eyes were motionless behind their lids this time. No mind, no R.E.M. sleep.

Image status healthy
18,216,369,102,558,196

Bill's mind: waiting in the cloud.

Image ready
Connectivity verified

"Ready when you are, my friend. When this is over, we're going out for drinks. But you're buying. Nod if that's okay with you."
Bill's body: toes up.

Proceed with image download? (y/n)

"Fine. I'll buy."
Victor pressed the key with authority.

Download initiated ...
Bytes copied: 1,530,088,084,637

The numbers farthest to the right of the screen were a blur as the byte count jumped at a rate of about 1.5 billion bytes per second. He stared at the number unblinkingly for about ten minutes until the byte count had climbed to a terabyte. It would take another three hours to download the complete image.

Bytes copied: 1,028,9▮▮▮▮▮▮▮▮▮▮▮

Bill lay there with his mind filling with information: childhood, education, adulthood, sexuality, experiences, downfalls, and everything else that made Bill Chevsky's who he was prior to his body's death; his first time riding a bike, first fight, first kiss, high school, college, marriage, the birth of his daughter, divorce, the death of his mother. It flooded into him as the same thoughts flooded into Victor's mind.

What would *his* image look like? How many bytes? How many bad sectors he wished he could erase from memory?

Image download successful
18,216,369,102,558,195

Three hours had passed, while the span of an entire life had transferred from cloud to man.

Checking downloaded image for inconsistences …

Something about the number didn't look right. Hair rose on the nape of Victor's neck. His stomach tightened. Compared to his notes, it was off by a single digit.

Image size mismatch of 1 byte

"I could have told you that," he said to the computer.

Array status healthy. No errors found
Size mismatch of 1 byte on downloaded image
Retry copy? (y/n)

He didn't have much of a choice. Instead of retrying the copy, Victor first checked the array for inconsistencies, and once more the computer told him the image stored on the cloud was fine, although a single byte larger in size than the downloaded version.

Retry copy? (y/n)

What could one byte matter?
Victor pounded the key this time.
It could be anything—a single one or a zero could matter more than anything!
He watched the screen the entire three hours, rarely moving his eyes away. His leg shook under the table, his palms sweaty. He was hungry and tired and had to pee but none of that mattered. He had bitten the insides of his gums raw and destroyed a majority of his fingernails by the time the image finished.

Image download successful
18,216,369,102,558,195

The same damn size. One single byte.
After repeated inconsistency checks on the hosted array image and the downloaded image, the computer greeted

him with the same annoying

Retry copy? (y/n)

"What do you think?" he asked Bill. "It's either going to work, or it's not going to work. If it's the latter, we still have the image stored on the cloud and we can retry downloading using a different machine, or try something else entirely. I'm talking to you like you can answer me. I'm losing it. I can't believe I'm talking to myself now and I'm losing it. What would you do if you were me, Bill?"

Bill was as eager as Victor for all of this to work. He'd say screw the single byte and try it anyway. What could it hurt?

He chose no after hesitating over the y key.

Image copy successful
Disconnect before rebooting patient

Victor disconnected the catheter at the back of Bill's head. It was a strange feeling, knowing he was going to reboot a human being, as if he were some kind of device instead of a living, breathing person. He remembered the term from history class at college. Bootstrapping, they used to call it. It was old computer terminology, when bootstrap buttons were pressed in order to initiate hardwired programs. It derived from the phrase "pulling oneself up by one's bootstrap," which of course was an impossible task. Even before that, the word bootstrap meant "to better oneself by one's own unaided efforts." Both seemed appropriate. Bill required Victor's help to get him out of the mud, and the goal was to better Bill's physical self.

He pressed the button that would normally shoot drugs into Bill's system to wake him up, but since he was comatose, it was simply the first step to rebooting his patient. The second step required the electromagnetic pulse to turn off the nano-technology in his system. Before doing this, Victor noticed movement behind Bill's eyes. They were shaking back and forth behind their lids. Bill Chevsky was in R.E.M. sleep. He was dreaming. He was in there.

Victor's experiment had worked. He had successfully re-imaged a human mind.

"Welcome back," he said, pressing the button to send the electromagnetic pulse.

Bill booted, his body jolting as if someone had shaken him awake.

He opened his eyes.

"Bill?"

His patient stared at the ceiling for a moment and then turned to him. He cleared his throat and shifted on the operating table. "Did it work?"

Victor smiled.

Bill cloned it.

And then he jolted again on the table and fell flat. He opened his eyes.

"Bill?"

His patient stared at the ceiling for a moment and then turned to him. He cleared his throat and shifted on the operating table. "Did it work?"

Victor smiled.

Bill cloned it.

And then he jolted again on the table and fell flat,

opened his eyes, and repeated the same process: the same throat clearing, the same shift on the table, the same question of whether or not the experiment had worked. He was on an endless cycle of rebooting.

Victor shook him, tried to snap him out of it, but nothing worked. After the third or fourth cycle, Victor's smile had turned to a look of confusion, and fear, and however Victor changed his expression, Bill matched it identically. Soon it became maddening. The jolt and the throat-clearing and the shift and the question—it never ended.

While Bill Chevsky continuously attempted the impossible task of pulling himself up by his own bootstraps, Victor checked the display on this monitor because it read something awful.

Image size mismatch

One byte.
Bill cleared his throat.

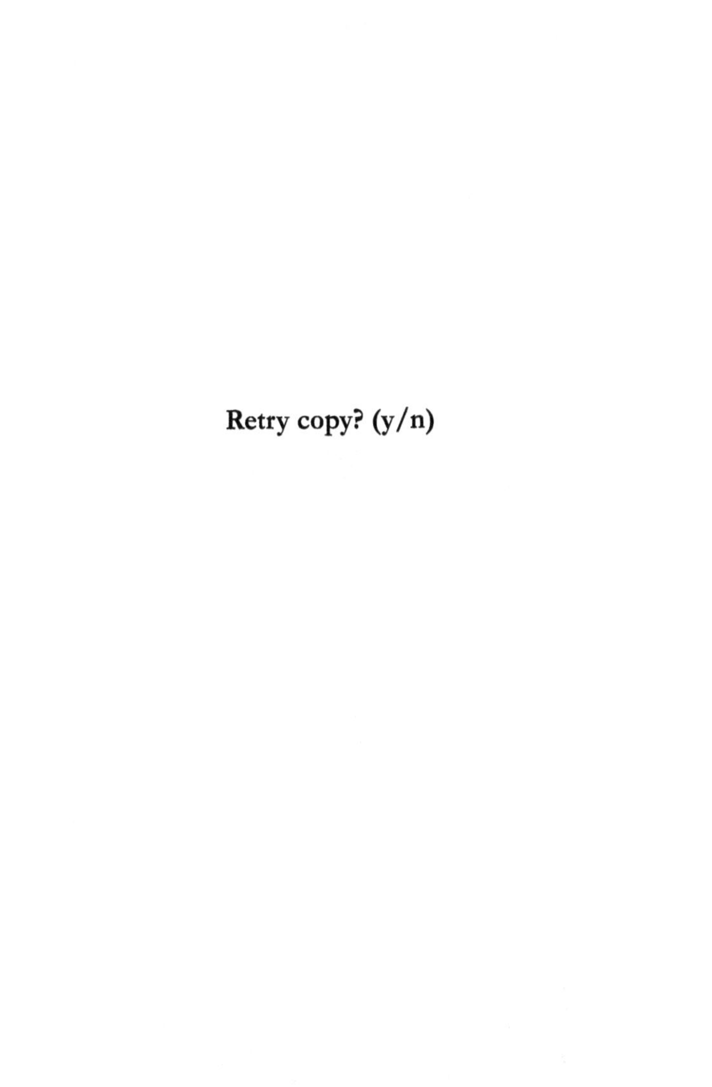

Retry copy? (y/n)

The Two of You

replicated
your plagiarized self
derivative, imitative, fake
and now there are two
one modified
heterogeneous, limited
incongruous
restricted by death
simple binary composition
digital makeup
zeros and ones
the two of you consider the doors
one to open
the zero to close
on and off, yes and no, life and loss
because there are two
you close the one
your way out, and your other's way in
you feel the dark
and embrace the light

A Light in the Closet

Bogey was in my room again last night. He was wearing a tan trench coat with a hood. He's tall, like my brother in the Army, and he drags his left foot across the floor when he walks because he probably got tank pieces blown at him from the war, too. Daddy says he isn't Jared because my brother died from the sand people. He says the man that hides in my closet is a boogeyman. I call him Bogey because that's how my dad pronounces it.

He wears boots. Dirty ones. I know they're dirty because he always leaves foot shapes on the carpet from the closet to my bed and then back to the closet. One set looks like it's made by a foot. The other's a smear because of how he walks. I clean it up in the mornings or I get in trouble. I think he has something dark covering his face, too.

I looked for a door in the back of my closet, but there isn't one. It must be magic, or maybe there's an invisible door hidden somewhere. He probably has a family too with a little girl like me having sleepovers in *his* closet.

Bogey visits at least once a week, but I don't see much of him because it's so dark and he's by himself in the closet. He sees me, though. Sometimes I see his eyes in the door crack if the moon's shining on him. They glow a really light blue, the way a cat's eyes will glow in the dark if light is on them. His eyes are the same as me and my brother's. Mostly he watches from inside the closet, but sometimes I hear him breathing over me or he takes my stuffed animals so he can smell them. I found Cali by my clothes hamper once—she's my baby bear—and she had a black hand on her neck and a nose print on her belly. I tried washing her, but his handprint wouldn't come off and I threw her away so Mom wouldn't find out.

Sometimes the closet door is closed and I wake up and see a blue door outline, probably from his eyes, and I hide under the covers because it's scary.

In the daytime, the closet holds my clothes, shoes, and all my other junk. Sometimes when I'm changing I wonder if he's hiding in there. I don't know how anyone can live in my closet, especially in the nighttime when it's dark. My stuff takes up most of the room. There are definitely places to hide, but it's very small in there and Bogey's big. There are two bars going across, one on each side to hang clothes, and a pull chain light in the middle of the room with a burnt-out bulb. Daddy's changed it a bunch of times, but he says there must be a short somewhere because it always burns out after a couple days.

Bogey must be scared of me. He never shows me his face and doesn't like to talk. He stands there most of the time with his arms swinging back and forth at his knees. I drew a picture of him once and my mom called him gangly. He's taller than my dad—and he's six-foot-three—even though he slouches like a question mark, like one of my stuffed animals. When it's quiet, I hear Bogey breathing like he's out of breath. Maybe his face is gross.

Sometimes when he's standing over me and I'm hiding under the covers I make believe what he looks like and I get more scared. I close my eyes and cover my ears and try to make him go away. I can tell he's in the room because it gets cold. Even if I can't hear him breathing, I can see air puffing out of the darkness like he's smoking Daddy's cigarettes. I peeked between my fingers one time because it got really cold and there was fog coming out of the blue line at the bottom of the closet door.

The first time I saw Bogey was after I woke up from a nightmare, which is why I know he's real. I remember dreaming that I was being chased by a werewolf through a field and I tripped over a rock, but it wasn't a rock at all but a skeleton head, all broken apart and smiling like a carved pumpkin, and the wolf was getting closer and when I screamed in the dream I woke up for real and Bogey was standing in front of my closet door. It was dark, but I could see the outline of the door and the outline of Bogey and he was watching me.

Daddy ran into my room and turned on the lights and saw me pointing a finger at the closet but Bogey was gone and I was only pointing at a closed door. He looked inside the closet for me and saw the light was on and said it was my mind playing tricks on me and that I should stop watching scary movies. After he turned off the flickering closet light and closed the door, he turned off the bedroom light as well and said to go back to sleep. I tried to close my eyes but I couldn't until I heard his door close. And then it got cold. Really cold. I never opened my eyes, but I remember a doorknob twisting and the closet door creaking, followed by limping steps into my room. I covered myself with my blanket so not a single part of me was showing.

Last night's probably the last night I'll ever see Bogey. A few minutes after Daddy kissed me goodnight and my mom kissed me goodnight and they turned off the light and left me alone, I got out of bed and walked in the dark to my closet. I opened the door and expected to see Bogey standing there with his glowing blue eyes. But it wasn't cold and he wasn't there. I pulled the chain and the light flickered because of the short. I felt for him. Only my clothes and junk were in there, though. I thought I touched his boots once, but they were my-sized boots.

I wanted to see Bogey with the lights on and tell him he wasn't a scary boogeyman and tell him he didn't have to hide his face anymore. Go home, I said. He was my angel all this time, the kind Daddy said should have been watching over Jared while he was in the Army. Bogey was trying to be my angel. It was my turn to watch *him* now. I didn't need an angel. He did.

Pulling the handle, the closet door creaked until it was open only a crack.

Inside the closet, I saw things through Bogey's eyes. The light flickered back on for a second and I saw he was standing next to my bed, looking out the window. He wore a tan trench coat with a hood. And boots. Dirty ones. He looked like Jared from the back. Foot shapes on the carpet led out from the closet that weren't there before, and also a long smear from his bad leg. If he turned around, he'd see an outline of light in the shape of a door, and me. He leaned over my bed and pulled something from his trench coat. He brought it to his nose and smelled it before setting it on the bed. Cali. She was clean. He had saved my baby bear.

When the light in the closet flickered off, he was gone.

Bogey

A rotting corpse wrapped in gunny
Watching me while I sleep
Mom says to stop, it's not funny
That I should count my sheep

The first time I told her, she cried
Don't lie to me, she said
I'm not, he's real, come see, I tried
He can't hurt me, he's dead

Bogey doesn't want to kill me
He only wants to play
My stuffed animals are fuzzy
He likes them, can he stay?

Imagination, my daughter
I'm turning off the light
Please don't make me get your father
Now I'm saying goodnight

She tucks me in, kisses my cheeks
Shuts the door, walks away
I smell him when the closet creaks
If my eyes close, he'll stay

He's dripping wet onto my bed
My teddy bears are stained
I see his hands are colored red
His neck, broken and craned

Bogey, won't you let me see you?
(Though fingers hide my fears)
I peek: his eyes, they glow so blue
Before he disappears

Mum

Fire eats her face, her shoulders, arms, hands, torso, and thighs. Fire eats all of her with an inhalation of hungry breath until her bedroom is void of air and the exhalation caused by an opened door draws the fire's attention elsewhere to feed. Away from Mum as she sleeps.

We have an important decision to make. Some call it pulling the plug, but it's not really pulling the plug; it's simply a button to push or a switch to switch and the connected device hums hums hums and then clicks to deathly silence as a risen chest falls one last time.

There's no power cord to yank from the wall. There is, but that won't kill her. These machines have battery backups to keep the machines living when they should otherwise be dead, which keep the living alive when they should otherwise be dead.

When we push the button or switch the switch on these machines, the lights go out—or burn out, perhaps—like a no-longer-hungry fire. The jumping jagged lines revealing life in digital form flatten, maybe tired and ready to move on, like the fire, or they fall flat one last time, like the chest.

We look at each other before looking to the machine that's keeping her alive.

The last thing you said to Mum before the fire was to stay out of your life, to stop asking about Emma. It doesn't matter why Emma left you. Mum knows that. She wanted to help you through the bad because she went through the bad with Dad, when he started seeing someone, when they were still together. Does it make you happy now? You told Mum to go away, to "literally burn in hell." Here she is, burned all to hell. Do you wonder if you did this to her? Where were you? Were you with Emma?

I watch her breathe and it helps me breathe: a slow rise, a slow fall; a click before every long exhale. The rhythm is stable and hypnotic and nearly puts me to sleep until the machine beeps, or starts to hiss as blood pressure is automatically taken, or when the nurse comes in to change bandages. Eighty-seven percent. That's how much of Mum is covered in bandages. The nurse, she tells me I'm going to need to learn how to change them.

Her skin, once black, is raw underneath the layers of gauze. Doctors, or surgeons, or whoever works on burn patients, peel away the burnt parts of Mum. Skin will not grow on dead skin, the nurse tells her, though she cannot hear any of these words.

Mum, she no longer has ears.

Her skin smells of lotion or ointment or whatever is put on burn patients. Some kind of minty emollient or gel / jelly substance she cannot smell.

Mum, she no longer has a nose.

The softest parts of the body burn first, the nurse tells her.

Even though we're told it might be best to leave, we stay through the changing.

The doctor, or surgeon, or whatever he is, the man with the white mask covering his face so he won't smell the horrible smells, he removes a red blotch and unwinds a once-white wrap, which coils to the stainless steel tray like a carefully placed snake. He doesn't want us to see the mess, but it's there: the yellow / red / brown mountain of skin-fused bandages. Coagulation.

"You should come back in an hour," he says. "This will take about an hour."

The machine silently blinks blinks blinks with a pulse. Blood pressure automatically takes as a plastic lung rises, stronger than the chest for which it breathes. After a slow exhalation hiss, a double-digit number over a smaller double-digit number displays on the screen and neither of us understands the meaning.

We stay.

A flame's only hungry if there's something new to burn. The smoking fireman in the front yard told you this an hour after you'd told Mum you'd be there. Once burnt, things no longer like to burn. A flame looks for something wet and moist, something new. A flame would rather devour a living tree and flourish than starve on a charcoaled husk of a tree and die. Fire would rather move from one trunk to the next, spreading through limbs, branches, and leaves: a viral fire. A damn social network of destruction.

Trunks: torsos. Limbs: arms. Branches: hands. Leaves: fingers.

It could have been both of you.

With Mum blackened and dry, the fire was done with her husk. The fire had moved on to drier things, like the kitchen, the bathroom, the front half of the house. Black seeped through exterior walls by the time the giant white snakes doused what was left of the roof. Smoke wafted from the soggy ashes the way it wafted from Mum when they wheeled her out.

You bummed a cigarette from the fireman, something new, let him light it from the ember of the one dangling from his mouth, then moved it to your lips. This something new, you carried the torch. Did you think about Mum, then, as you inhaled the smoke?

The handheld breathing device covering her face as they wheeled her out then, the paramedic at her side squeezing regulated air into and out of her lungs …

The machine at her side, plugged into the battery-backed power, it pumps air into and out of her lungs instead of a man, breathing for her, keeping her alive because she can't do it on her own …

Do you think about assisted breathing when you leave her side every hour on the hour to find 'fresh air' outside the patient waiting room as you spread fire and billow smoke, or do you wonder about the house and what the insurance will cover?

I rode with her to the hospital. Mum's red and charred-raw hand, it stuck to me as I held onto what was left of a fading grip that barely held back. I'd squeeze, and she'd squeeze. I'm here for you Mum, I'd say. When paramedics rolled her away, her skin stuck, adding another layer to my own, as frail as black tissue paper.

I rode with her to the hospital …

Her body is jerky: dried in the heat, shrunken, brownish-red.

There are degrees and she's mostly third. The third-degree is what peels away like weathered paint. The third degree involves all layers of the skin, or epidermis, as the pamphlet says. The charred areas that used to be her epidermis, and the dry white areas, some of this clings to her burned clothes to form a new layer of skin. A special blend of cotton-polyester-epidermis.

She should have the burnt parts elevated above her heart, the pamphlet says, but there's no proper way to raise eighty-seven percent of her body above her heart.

Her other thirteen percent, this part of Mum is a mix of first and second-degree burns, according to the pamphlet. The blisters and the intensely red and splotchy parts: second. The lighter red and swelling: first. The little yellow book also says burns are susceptible to tetanus, but Mum hasn't been to the hospital since she last gave birth.

She's still alive. She must want to live for a reason. There must be something she wants to get off her chest besides the skin, something left to say.

We remove the expired gauze as the nurse instructs. We do this when the white goes away, when the red seeps seeps seeps through to the surface, but only when the blood starts to dry and turn brown. Like the fire, the bandages look for something wet and moist, something new, while the blood they soak searches for the opposite. Blood would rather move from one bandage to the next, spreading through gauze after gauze after gauze: a viral bleeding. A damn social network of red blood cells escaping the body while white blood cells stick around to help.

The old gauze, we coil it on the stainless steel tray. The new gauze, we make it moist with some kind of minty emollient or gel / jelly substance, the same stuff we spatula onto Mum's open wounds. This makes them look worse.

White blood cells are leukocytes, the nurse tells us, as if that means anything at all. After we both offer a "don't understand" expression, she tells us that leukocytes are part of the immune system. Blood pools to a wound so it can help fight infection. The little white warriors are there to help. The snot that runs down our nose, that's mostly white blood cells. When we pick our nose, we're mostly picking dried white blood cells. When our children eat what they find up there, they're learning to become albino vampires.

Mum's nurse thinks she has a sense of humor.

We silently watch a demonstration of things we need to learn.

The endless white bandages, they go round round

round her arms and legs as we lift, winding up her thighs to the place that brought us into this world, around her ankles and wrists; the bandages climb her neck. After dabbing ointment on the red half-moons under her eyes where there used to be bags, we cover the wounds on her face.

"She's in a coma," the nurse says, "though some believe she can hear your words."

We give Mum silence and sit her upright.

"This requires two," the nurse says.

One of us holds her up while the other unwinds the old bandages from her chest and winds on the new.

The more we layer, the less seeps through.

You bring Emma to see Mum like she's part of the family. You bring her in and the two of you sit across from the bed, watching; not helping, but watching, wanting to say good-bye. You stroke the back of Emma's hand like she's some kind of pet, a purring cat. You watch your sister take Mum's hand, cautious of the wound.

I read an article once …

Cats will eat the soft parts of the face first if left alone long enough with the dead. Domesticated cats starve because they cannot feed themselves. They rely on the dead to feed them, and they resort to eating faces. This article, the words make me think of the hungry fire that ate Mum's ears and nose, the droopy bags that once hung below her eyes, as well as her lips and the soft skin outlining what used to be her smile.

I read an article once that domesticated cats were worshiped by ancient Egyptians and seen as symbols of poise and grace. These poised and graceful face-eating cats, they sometimes received the same mummification as their owners. The cat goddess, Bast or Bastet or something like that, she was the deity of things like motherhood, protection and fertility.

The bandages, they cover a majority of Mum's body.

I read an article once …

White wrappings preserve her while she sleeps the long sleep. The blood does its work underneath: white cells fighting for her life while the red watch her die. One of her daughters is like the red; the other is like the white. One of her daughters wants to leave the figurative plug plugged into the wall for as long as it takes; the other wants to pull.

She resembles a cocoon. Mum underneath, ready for metamorphosis, she is ready to pass from this life to the next.

We argue until we're no longer sisters.

You don't want her alive. You want her plugged in, but that's not really living; that's a CPR dummy mocking life while someone else does the breathing.

"Goodbye, Mum," you say, and kiss her bandaged brow.

Emma, she pulls your hand to let you know it's time to go.

I want her to live, so I pull the plug.

At four in the morning, the hospital sleeps. All is quiet but for the gentle hum of the machine doing the breathing. All is dark but for a few florescent lights, the soft green glow of exit signs spotting the hall, the jumping jagged lines revealing life in digital form.

"Goodbye, Mum," I say, and kiss her bandaged brow.

I squeeze her hand to let her know it's time to go.

It's not really pulling the plug, but pushing a button and the connected device hums hums hums and then clicks to deathly silence. A risen chest falls one last time.

The machine, when I push the button, the lights go out, and I'm reminded of the no-longer-hungry fire I had set. The machine, it's done with Mum. The jumping jagged lines revealing life in digital form flatten, tired, ready to move on; they fall flat one last time.

"Hello, Mum," I say, and change her bandages.

Her body sits upright.

Sticks and Bones

A log head
Knots for eyes
Nible hands
Puny thighs

Should be fed
Stomach lies
No demands
Only ties

Bark skin shed
Bad disguise
Shaking hands
Despite tries

Sap is bled
Wooden cries
Hope withstands
Stick girl dies

Skinny

"Have you ever seen a smiling face
that wasn't beautiful?" – Mum

February – 184 lbs.

Lisa steps on the scale, her first time since high school. She's alone in her dorm room and allows the tears to fall, dripping onto the driver's license in her hand that reads five-foot-four, a hundred fifteen pounds. Never did she suspect one-eighty-four, sixteen pounds shy of the double century mark.

Maybe one-thirty-five, but not—

Time for a diet. Almost seventy pounds to lose. Seventy!

Lisa steps off the scale and faces her reflection, a sad image, her eyes dark and leaking like an old faucet. She slaps herself hard across the face. Red fingers stay behind.

She was pretty and petite once, a time when she could eat fast food for every meal and not gain an ounce, when metabolism was on her side. Now everything she eats turns to fat as she troughs it down.

She removes her clothes and reweighs herself naked,

disgusted by her image: rolls, cellulite, cottage cheese thighs.

Two lousy pounds. Sixty-eight to go.

She weighed sixty-eight pounds when she was ten.

This time next month the scale will show ten less, she tells herself. Ten pounds per month. Not a bad goal. Exercise, eat right, and in no time the fat will fall right off and you'll be skinny again.

March – 188 lbs.

A pound of fat is roughly the size of a softball, her mother once told her.

Lisa imagines four of them smashed around her belly. She grabs her stomach with both hands.

There's a text message on her phone from her mother: *Lisa, haven't talked to you in a while. Everything okay? Not pregnant, are you? Lol.*

Pregnant?

There *was* that time with Brayson Mills a couple months ago, but her last—

She tries to remember her last period, checks under the sink to count her feminine products, and returns with a home pregnancy test she bought the last time she missed her period.

Her hands shake as she reads the instructions on the box for the second time in her life. It says to pee on the strip and she does. It says to wait the allotted time and she does. It's the longest sixty seconds of her life. As soon as the time expires, she peeks between her fingers. A pink line materializes, confirming her pregnancy.

No, no, no!

She imagines a future as a young mother in college trying to juggle a newborn. She'd lose her friends and would probably have to drop out, maybe move back in with her parents, work three jobs to buy diapers and whatever else babies needed. Lisa reads the instructions on the box to be sure.

1) Remove pregnancy test from package;

2) Remove plastic strip illustrated by figure A;

3) Urinate in designated area;

4) Wait one minute (sixty seconds, it states in parentheses) for results; and a conjured

5) Pray to the gods.

Underneath the five-step plan is a diagram that dumbs it down further:

+ Pregnancy Plausible
– Pregnancy Implausible

Pregnancy Implausible!

She looks at the pink dash, the pink hyphen, the pink minus symbol, whatever one would choose to call such a great symbol of relief. She slaps herself again for reading it wrong. That single pink line symbolizes many things for Lisa, like never having unprotected sex again, or at least being more careful with Brayson—vetoing it altogether while in college—or never having to worry about gaining baby weight.

Lisa smiles at her reflection. For once in these last few months, she is able to find happiness in something, even something as unfortunate as a pregnancy scare.

Her smile fades as she realizes her weight gain is a mystery.

Another text from her mother: *Call me, K?*

April – 188 lbs.

No loss; no gain.

Lisa allots three fast food trips this week, four less (maybe more) than the norm, and stays away from upsizing her greasy meals. She drinks soda, but that will soon change when she starts cutting carbohydrates; that's the trend, counting them, writing them down like sacred text and working the equation to reach an implausible sum of zero.

Next month will be salads instead of burgers, apple slices instead of fries, diet sodas instead of regular. The pounds will drop.

May – 180 lbs.

Eight pounds! Lisa shrills at the lighter person in the reflection. There is no difference in appearance, but the digital meter is never wrong. Technically, she started her diet at one eighty-four, but eight pounds lost is eight pounds lost. Best of all, she's followed the stricter diet of cutting back the carbohydrates, and cautious of her food intake in general.

Sixty-five pounds remain to reach her high school weight.

You'll lose that next month, she tells herself.

Lose?

To lose something you must misplace something. It was her mother that told her that one, too. But what she's trying to lose is something she created from scratch: fat. She hasn't misplaced anything.

After the weigh-in, Lisa hits the library and flips through the pages of a book about the Atkins diet. She learns not to cut *some* of her carbohydrates, but to cut *all* of them. Meats, cheeses, fats—those are good to go; pastas, sweets, breads, starches—those are mortal sins. This is how she interprets the book, at least. People *just like her* losing ten, twenty, even forty pounds per month by simply eliminating carbohydrates and not worrying about the other crap.

Lisa closes the book and puts it back.

On her walk home, she sees an advertisement for Herbalife. LOSE WEIGHT NOW, ASK ME HOW, it reads, followed by someone's number. She writes it down.

Another text from her mother, who used to sell Herbalife when Lisa was in middle school: *I'm starting to worry, Lisa. Please call. Love you.*

June – 161 lbs.

Lisa imagines a basket filled with nineteen softball sized chunks of her fatty tissue—what she's lost this last month—and it makes her happy, yet sick to her stomach.

So hungry …

Cutting carbohydrates from her diet has worked wonders. She sees the difference: stomach slimming, legs thinning, bra less snug. Her neck has thinned out, her cheeks less plump.

The hunger in her belly talks to her often.

She imagines Chinese take-out boxes around her. Ghost smells haunt her nose: egg rolls, chow mein, chow fun, fried rice, beef and broccoli, General Tso's chicken, kung pao anything. Suddenly she's dizzy, nauseated. She leans to the garbage can and pukes the imaginary food and whatever else was in her stomach.

She weighs herself again: an even one-sixty.

Never bulimia.

The smiling woman in the mirror lifts Lisa's shirt and calls her fat.

Nineteen pounds; nearly two-thirds of a pound lost per day. She'll be down to a hundred forty-something next month.

Her cell phone rings again, but she lets it go to voice-mail.

July – 152 lbs.

Nine more, yet she wonders what happened to the hundred forty-something she promised herself. Lisa weighs herself again in case the scale is wrong. It reads one-fifty-two.

She buys another one and it reads one-fifty-two.

She cries most of the night.

Next month her reflection will be thinner.

August – 148 lbs.

Six months. Thirty-six pounds. Not bad.

Is that how the diet works? A big chunk of weight loss and then a gradual slow down? If only she'd purchased the book instead of skimming through it. She'll give it a month and try another diet if the pounds stop dropping.

September – 145 lbs.

Lisa calls the toll free number she jotted down a few months ago. LOSE WEIGHT NOW, ASK ME HOW. An outlandishly hyperactive lady spiels for almost an hour about herbs being the healthy way to go, how she and her husband have been with the program for almost two years. This lady's husband lost sixty-two pounds and she lost twenty. Completely natural, she says. The weight will come off fast at first, and then gradually taper off until a healthy weight is reached.

Lisa orders two hundred dollars' worth of snack bars, shakes, protein powders, pills … the complete package deal. There's even a powder to mix in with her drinks to increase metabolism and provide energy.

For the next month, she has a shake for breakfast (chocolate, strawberry, or vanilla), half of a snack bar (to settle her stomach), a handful of colorful pills for lunch, followed by the second half of the snack bar, and a protein shake for dinner. And the powder—a legal form of speed when broken down chemically—mixed in with her drinks.

She does this for thirty days.

October – 133 lbs.

Twelve pounds have fallen and Lisa has never felt so alive. She forgets about the 30-day money back guarantee and places a second order.

November – 124 lbs.

The diet is not as triumphant, but Lisa's lost another nine of those unwanted pounds. Nine pounds shy of her goal weight.

People approach her now to tell her how great she looks.

Have you lost weight? You look amazing. What's your secret?

A cute guy in biology class asks her out on a date, her first in a while.

Finally, her life is changing.

Lisa undresses in front of the mirror.

Skinny! Almost as skinny as she was in high school. Her breast size is down at least a cup, but she can see her ribs and it makes her smile. Her hips and thighs are emaciated and beautiful, her stomach flat, face carved like a starving model's. None of her clothes fit, but that's a good thing. Just like the girls in the magazines.

Your waist is no longer a waste, her reflection tells her.

In seven months she's lost sixty-one pounds, a gym bag filled with softballs. The thought makes her queasy. She weighed sixty-one pounds in third grade.

December – 120 lbs.

Four …

Brayson calls, but she lets it go to voicemail.

She cries for the first time in months.

January – 119 lbs.

A single fucking pound.

Lisa steps off the scale and meets herself at the mirror. She slaps her face as hard as she can, enough to bruise later. The woman in front of her shows no emotion. She circles around and sees fat: hips too broad, thighs too thick, a backside hanging too far out, rolls in her sides, a plump stomach, a "waste."

This woman has become an evil little liar.

There are other diets you can try, she says.

Whichever is fastest, she tells her bony / obese reflection.

The underweight / overweight image tells her that fasting will be quickest, that she should only eat as a last resort of starvation. Protein only. No carbohydrates. Drink water to clench the appetite. Can't gain weight if you don't eat.

Lisa fasts for the entire next month and her body eats what it can to survive.

February – 110 lbs.

Her stomach is in knots, her midsection cramping and twisting into pretzel shapes. She's on her tenth glass of water for the day and it's only noon. She's peed five times and needs to go again.

Lisa's surpassed her goal weight by five pounds, but doesn't care.

Five pounds of unnecessary fat, she tells her reflection.

She has another date with the guy from biology class,

Elliot Harper. They've been dating on and off for fourteen pounds.

She gauges everything by her weight now, even time. Every day Elliot tells her how beautiful she is, leaves her notes, sends her texts. Every day he tells her she doesn't need to lose weight. It worries him sometimes that she is so thin.

What the fuck does he know?

Elliot's starting to sound like Brayson.

He tries to fatten her up by taking her to dinner and the movies—typical dates—but Lisa finds excuses for not eating. She passes on popcorn at the theatres, as well as candy and soda. I'll just have some of yours, she tells him, but then she never does.

Her mother, her roommate, Brayson, and now Elliot … what do they know? Every last one of them is overweight. Half the planet is overweight. More people die from obesity-related issues than from most diseases.

An entire year has passed, she realizes.

There's another text from her mother.

March – 102 lbs.

Hey Lisa, it's Brayson, listen … the text reads. She doesn't read any more of the message before deleting it. Her cell phone's littered with similar messages from all of them, her mother especially: *Call me*, and *We need to talk*, and *I'm worried about you* …

Lisa admires the beautiful young woman in the mirror and laughs at the thought of her desired weight of one-fifteen. Jawbones now accentuate her face. She hides her deep sockets with eye shadow and mascara. She's gone down from a size twenty to a size two. Her fellow students gawk with jealousy.

It's all part of being beautiful, her reflection tells her. She removes her clothes and stands naked, revealing a malnourished figure composed of skin and bone, a prominent ribcage and pelvic bones, dwindling muscles, hips and knees jutting in points, anorexic arms and twig legs. A figure with many shadows. A figure many women would die for.

April – 96 lbs.

She'd slap herself if she knew her face wouldn't bruise.

Elliot broke up with her, said she had to stop with the diets or he'd end their relationship—and so he did. But so what? Some guys dig skinny girls. And fuck him.

Her roommate, behind Lisa's back, scheduled an appointment for her with one of the school counselors, said she was worried about Lisa's health and that she was going to shrink down to nothing. Starving herself, she told him. Fuck her too.

The world was suddenly against her.

Clothes, too. She's practically swimming in her tops, and soon she'll no longer need a bra. Constantly wasting money on new clothes to fit the new Lisa …

Lastly, her body has turned against her and is constantly fighting the hunger. She's stopped counting glasses of water, and has to force herself to eat, usually a small salad chased with supplements and energy drinks.

Lisa undresses in front of the mirror.

Some guys dig skinny girls, she reminds herself.

May – 92 lbs.

Lisa cries against her pillow and it hurts because she's so fragile.

She is exactly half the weight at which she originally started … back when she weighed a hefty one eighty-four.

Half.

She thinks of softball-sized chunks of fatty tissue and visualizes ninety-two of them collected in a bathtub. She imagines her old self, split directly down the middle.

It took her roommate storming out, her boyfriend leaving—both of them—and eventual meetings with the counselor and finally her doctor for her to realize she had a problem. For two months now, she's missed her period, but not from pregnancy, Doctor Keppler informed her. It was simply from not ovulating.

You are going to die, Lisa! was the last thing her roommate said to her before leaving. And she was right. She was going to die.

Wiping tears from her eyes, Lisa drives to a place she's avoided for over a year—a fast food restaurant. She orders a double bacon cheeseburger, large fries, and a shake, forces the food down, and reads the nutritional information on the tray mat. Her entire meal is 1,840 calories, mostly from fat, with seventy-two grams of carbohydrates and over three grams of sodium. A heavenly meal. An entire day's worth of—

And then her stomach lurches and the food exorcizes from her body like a food demon. She collapses onto the mess.

June – 84 lbs.

For a month, Lisa tries—and tires—to eat, and to date.

The best she manages is two "normal" meals per day, one of which her body rejects—usually the earlier meal, which is good for her social life. No guy wants to be with a woman at a candle light dinner excusing herself to the restroom between drinks to throw up. But it happens.

It's not bulimia, she tells herself, if she doesn't *want* it to happen. Bulimia is something sought after, something controlled, fingers shoved down throats. This is something different. Her body simply refuses to be hungry, her appetite is gone, and when she *is* hungry, or forces herself to eat, what goes in instantly wants out.

Her body has accommodated to malnourishment.

Pills go down, vitamins, supplements and fat burners and whatnot, but sometimes they make her sick. So she takes pills to settle her stomach. Everything makes her sick, even water. She drinks gallons, mostly to give herself a false acceptance of "full." You drink a lot of water, her last date tells her, some nerdy guy in a tie. He *is* her last, she realizes. She can't do this anymore …

Hydration, she says before excusing herself to the ladies room.

Lisa leans over the toilet and waits for it to happen, her stomach churning the few bites of salad and bread. Two minutes pass, although she's spit into the bowl a few times expecting more.

It's not bulimia, she tells herself, pushing her middle finger into her throat, if she doesn't *want* it to happen. She bites onto the third knuckle of that finger and pushes hard against her uvula until it happens: the purging of the food that doesn't want to be in her stomach.

The next thing she knows, she's at his place.

For the last time, she reminds herself.

She undresses in front of him, but the lights are off. It's been a while since she's felt *wanted* by anyone, let alone for sex, although she realizes the lights will eventually have to be turned back on, exposing her shadows and what she's become.

Some guys dig skinny girls, she reminds herself, although she knows now this is a lie. It's a *fetish*, Lisa realizes. Sick guys dig sick girls.

Lisa lets him dig until shame leaks down her leg. She stays with him until he's asleep. Under the cover of darkness, her bruises well hidden, she gets dressed and leaves, wondering how many calories were burned and whether or not he'd leave messages like the others. At least pregnancy's not a concern, she muses, since ovulation's out of the picture.

July – 80 lbs.

Lisa cries herself to sleep each night.

She dreams of someday learning to eat again. She dreams of gaining a hundred and four pounds to be at her original weight, but realizes each time she wakes that such a task is impossible.

She wants to stand in front of the mirror and tell her skeletal reflection that she was wrong all along, but she can no longer stand to look at that woman. She's repulsive.

She weighs herself daily, by the ounce, for any sign of gain. She hopes others with her condition find the courage to stand up, as she is unable to do even that now, to rise out of bed, to get help. She's scared to death that in the end hope is a mirage.

August – 79 lbs, 12 oz.

September – 79 lbs, 3 oz.

October – 78 lbs, 6 oz.

November – 78 lbs, 0 oz.

The last time Lisa weighed seventy-eight pounds, she was twelve years old and bragging to her schoolmates about growing up to be six feet tall and weighing hundreds and hundreds of pounds ... bigger than all of them.

She flips through the pages of her middle school yearbooks now, remembering those days, what she liked to refer to as the *innocent* years.

None of her friends ever dreamed of starved-prominent cheekbones, of bony ribcages, of twig-like arms and legs, of flat chests, of vomiting and pain.

I want to grow up to be just like you, she used to tell her mother.

And the hugs that followed were always heavenly.

Closing the book, Lisa hides her innocent past.

Twenty-three missed messages from her mother fill the notification area on her cell phone, as well as thirteen missed calls. There are others from her once-roommate, and even a voicemail from Brayson long ago she could never come to delete. *Hey, just wanted you to know I was thinking about you*, it would probably say if she willed herself to play it. She sets the phone to Silent and takes in the quiet.

She hadn't spoken to any of them for as long as she could remember.

Her mother … had it been over a year? Two?

December – 77 lbs. 9 oz.

Another text from her mother: *Have you ever seen a smiling face that wasn't beautiful?* The screen of the cell phone reflects Lisa's smile and she wonders if it's true.

January – 75 lbs, 4 oz.

Lisa reads the message again, sets the phone aside. A hundred pounds ago; that was the last time they had spoken. She considers calling, but it hurts too much to think of what to say. She considers sending a text: *Mum, I don't know how to—*

February – 68 lbs. 2 oz.

Without reading any of the messages, without listening to any of the voicemails, Lisa deletes them all. She takes her phone off Silent for the first time in months.

She scrolls through the contacts on her cell phone to the only one without a first and last name, the one simply labeled *Mum*.

It's time to say goodbye.

Her mother answers midway through the first ring and says the opposite.

March –

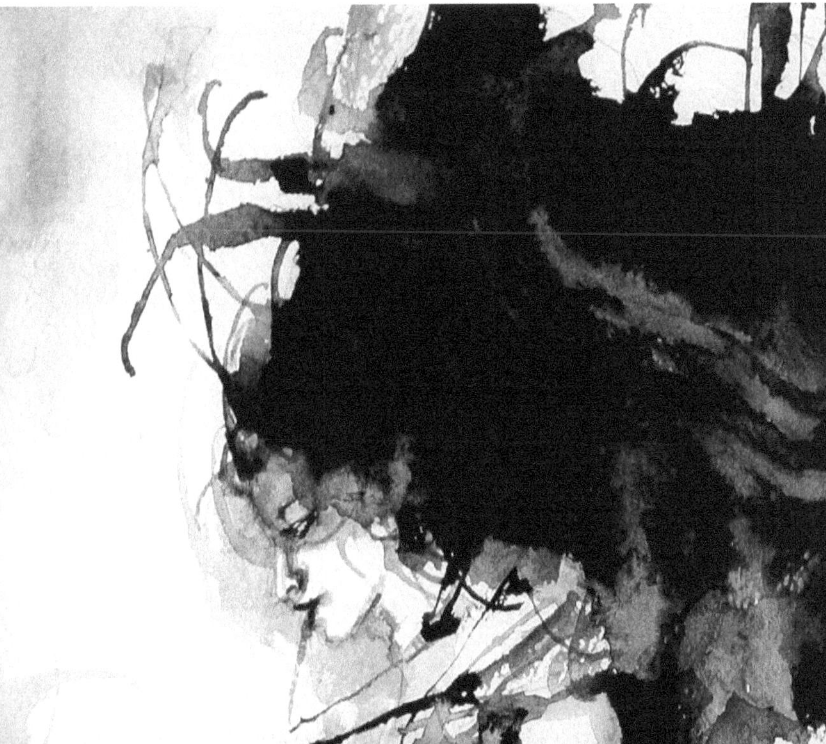

Void

Not the Child

Her wings were sharp and shimmering white and four times her size. The faerie was no more than a foot tall, and naked, her skin also white and translucent. She flew in spurts and perched on the traffic signal, wings outstretched.

I watched this creature from my downtown apartment while pregnant. I assumed it was all in my head at first, something fantastic my mind had conjured to transport me away from the thought of carrying a child.

I was wrong.

She tucked her wings and fell onto a businessman waiting to cross the street, fluttering as she landed on his shoulder. Curious hands played with his ear while she looked inside his head. Tiny fingers pulled at something dark inside. The man was oblivious as she pulled out a smoky substance that pooled on the concrete. An ethereal body materialized from the ground up: feet, followed by legs, a torso, arms, and a head, all of which she tugged out of his ear. Soon the man had a ghostly twin.

When the crosswalk light changed from an amputated hand to a walking man, the faerie flapped her wings and hovered. She held onto what I thought was his soul with both hands. The man's body stayed behind and walked in the opposite direction while his shadow walked in place, gripped by this beautiful thing with wings. A thin line of dark matter reeled out of his ear.

Despite thinking a person's soul would be weightless, she carried it with burden, the way I'd carry a suitcase made for giants if I had wings and could fly. She was quite beautiful with the early sun casting light upon her body.

The faerie struggled outside my window as the gray line, anchored to the man on the ground, pulled taut. She looked my way for a moment with her glowing eyes, but I could tell she couldn't see me.

I followed the trailing substance to the man on the ground as she pumped her enormous wings, stretching the cord, and then it snapped and she flew out of sight, a length of gray trailing behind.

The soulless man on the ground staggered a few steps before collapsing.

Moments later, he was surrounded. A woman on a cellular waved frantically for help as a man in a suit passed by undisturbed. A young man with scraggly hair let his bicycle crash as he jumped from it and knelt next to the fallen body. The cyclist searched for a pulse as spectators amassed.

Like a silent film, I watched from my apartment. I reached for my phone, but realized a few on the street were already calling for help.

The cyclist performed compressions and mouth-to-mouth resuscitation until the ambulance arrived. With exception to the medics, he was the only one who offered assistance.

A dozen surrounded this poor fellow; they all wanted to watch.

The ambulance left with lights flashing and sirens blaring. Show over, the crowd dispersed—all but the cyclist. He sat on the sidewalk and stayed a while, exhausted, looking in the direction of the ambulance. He finally rose, retrieved his crumpled bike from the curb, and rode away.

The child inside pushed against a rib.

I wrapped myself in a blanket and held her close.

I woke to a disturbance outside my window later that night when I got up to pee. The squealing of tires brought me to the window, as well as the revving of an engine and a glimpse of taillights dissolving into the street. Two women argued over whoever had sped off in the black sports car. A lonely streetlight illuminated the two women in dim orange. The smaller one held a knife. They exchanged rapid Spanish, but I only understood two words: *puta* and *dinero*.

I suddenly craved Mexican; that's pregnancy for you. Two glowing embers from the other side of the street watched a reversed image of what I could see. The faerie. I saw only her eyes. She perched on the ledge of the building opposite mine. She waited, I knew, for the chaos of life to give her work—to take one of these women if the fight between them worsened. To *where* was the mystery. She'd swoop onto one of their shoulders and pull out the darkness.

Swearing led to slapping led to hair-pulling led to wrestling led to the larger of the women choking on blood with the hilt of a knife sticking from her chest. She wheezed from pierced lungs, holding her stomach, trying to cover more stab wounds than she had fingers. The other woman rambled off a string of words not in my vocabulary before getting into a beat-up Nissan Sentra and driving away.

I called 911.

The woman filled with holes moved onto her back, her panicked face searching for air like a bloodied trout slapping on the shore. She tried to sit upright, but collapsed as the faerie descended from her dark hiding space across the street.

"What's your emergency?"

Under the streetlight, the creature's eyes lost luminescence. White wings fluttered as she landed on the dying woman's chest; outstretched, the wings were nearly the length of the entire woman's body. How the faerie's small figure could support such a weight had my mind reeling. The uneven surface under her feet rose and fell as the woman under her tried to breathe. Erupting wounds spattered the small body red.

"I need to report a—"

The creature stood over the dying woman, looking into her mouth, reaching into it with delicate hands, pulling.

"Miss?"

Little did the faerie know, I watched from my apartment.

An assault, I wanted to say, but that wasn't the right word.

The creature slowly pulled something the size of a garbage bag from the woman's throat. It lay next to the lady in a lump, like a giant, black, cancerous lung, and it took a while to realize I was staring at a shadowy replica of the dying woman. Holding an end of it with her delicate hands, the faerie pumped her wings, rose to the air and flew away with a line of black trailing behind her. It was taut for a moment, and then snapped near the stabbed woman's mouth. The woman convulsed and her life ended.

"A murder."

The naked white faerie with the bat wings flew away, body splotched in the blood of the dead, clutching the black mass that had once lived inside the profane woman's body. She faded into the night with the shadow of a kite string trailing behind.

I explained what I had seen: two women fighting, one pulling a knife on the other and stabbing, the other driving away.

Yes, the woman was dead, I said. Yes, I was sure. No, I wouldn't go down to check, and yes, I would stay in my apartment. The car was a silver Nissan Sentra, I told her, but I couldn't recall the plates.

A police cruiser parked a far distance away from the dead woman. It had taken nearly thirty minutes. Two officers inspected the body with flashlights and spoke into radios on their collars. A crime scene unit arrived to take pictures, followed by a van. They bagged her up and drove away.

This was the city in which I lived.

This was the city I so desired to leave.

As a soon-to-be single parent, I didn't have much of a choice but to stay.

Something the size of a crow hit my window months later, but I knew it wasn't a bird of any kind. My previous tummy bump resembled a basketball shoved under my blouse, and

I supported that extra weight as I admired my semi-transparent reflection. I looked through myself to the white smear the faerie had made.

She hit the window a second time, wings fluttering against the glass. Like a moth's phototactic attraction to light, she frantically struck the window over and over again, wanting inside. It was the middle of the day and she wanted in. She managed to grasp the bottom frame of the window with clawed toes, her hands slapping the glass and staying there, wings pumping just enough to hold her body upright. Up close, she was both beautiful and terrifying: smooth white skin, thin, ill-proportioned wings too big for her body, an angelic face, small jagged teeth, and wide scarlet eyes. Definitely female.

Her small lungs panted.

I put my hand against the glass so that our hands met—her entire hand smaller than my thumb—and noticed her glowering at my stomach.

No.

As I moved, her eyes followed the hand supporting my belly.

I smacked the glass hard and she fluttered away, only to return, slapping against the window. Clawed fingers created four parallel marks on the glass.

Not once did she look at my face.

I stepped back as she repositioned, gripping the top of the window with her tiny hands, her feet pushing off, body swinging, feet slamming against the window.

"Stay away from my child."

She flew away, as if adhering to my words.

"That's right."

She slammed into the window again.

No!

I hit the glass with a balled fist and that's when she noticed me. She cowered. Something about me had scared her, maybe an aura of color I had released—like the smoky substance escaping the bodies of the souls she took. For I could tell she didn't see me the same way I saw her. Jerky eyes searched the room for what had pounded against the glass, head swiveling rapidly. She knew I was there, but I was invisible.

Her work was the child ... and only the child.

The child inside doubled me over in pain and whatever color I projected scared the creature enough that it flew away.

"Not the child."

The woman in front of me in the checkout stand turned her head and admired my stomach and the items in my cart before minding her own business. I couldn't blame her for the curiosity; what I had said sounded strange coming from the mouth of a pregnant woman.

"How far along are you?"

"Thirty weeks."

"Boy or girl?"

"A girl, I think."

She left it at that and I was relieved she didn't ask about the man in my life, since the man in my life had left the same night he'd put this life inside me. I was thirty weeks along and hadn't returned to the doctor to determine the sex of the—

"My god," said the woman. She said it casually, and then she said it a second time dramatically and with a hand to her mouth; her other hand pointing to the rose blossoming from the middle of my sweatpants, blood running the length of my legs.

I saw the little faerie creature as I fell to the floor. She admired the mess from atop a pile of paper bags, wings folded behind her back.

The checker said something into the phone mounted on the pole next to the register, but I couldn't decipher the garble over the loudspeaker. The woman in front of me opened a roll of paper towels she planned to purchase and wadded them around me, avoiding touching my blood. She shoved more toward me and then stepped away to make a call, like the woman I had seen in the street. Others in the store scrambled to my aid but stayed far away. They were afraid of what they were seeing. My eyes stayed on what they *couldn't* see.

"Everything will be okay," said the woman on the phone.

Nothing would be okay.

"Not the child," I said again. "Please, not the child."

The child pooled around me.

My child's white faerie glanced to the rafters where a second creature had perched, waiting patiently for fate to unfold, like her wings, which disentangled. Side-by-side the two were identical, twin-like: one to take my child's life, the other to take mine.

I felt my life draining my child's.

The second faerie flapped her wings, body outstretched. Dainty feet touched down beside me. The other joined on the opposite side.

No!

I managed to kick the one on my right, but the other jumped onto my legs and held me down and I lay paralyzed, her clawed feet somehow holding me down without piercing my skin. She stood on me as if I were nothing more than a ledge upon which she perched. Her touch kept me immobile. She bent over the red between my legs and pulled out the gray. I watched her pull out the child, my nameless child, with delicate infant features periodically showing through her soul cloud.

And then the faerie flew away with the life of my unborn child.

"Have some water," said the checker, holding a bottle in front of me.

"I called for an ambulance," said the woman who had placed the call. She took the bottle from him, kneeled next to me, unscrewed the cap and lifted the back of my head. Water poured over my mouth and down my face.

I was the only one who saw them.

The second faerie eagerly advanced.

I zapped the hell out of the little white creature with myTaser before she could lay her claws on me. I'd kept it in my purse since becoming single. Her body went into spasms and curled into a fetal position. I held her scrawny neck to the floor and smashed the Taser against her skull, over and over again.

To those around me, it must have looked like the woman who'd just miscarried took out her frustrations on the first thing she found in her purse.

Gray leaked from what was left of a once beautiful being and evaporated. Her white body started to darken, still writhing in what looked like convulsions. I grabbed each of her wings and ripped them from her slender body and it was like tearing at tissue paper—like cotton candy dissolving against wet fingertips.

That's when I noticed the moth. The common insect fluttered toward the dying faerie and landed on her shoulder, there to take her away.

I don't remember the ambulance ride to the hospital, or much of anything after the moth; but I thought about the paralysis and whether it was the first faerie's touch that had put me there … or fear. Either way, I was unable to save my child. Only myself.

Never had I bled so heavily. To think that it was the life of either my daughter or my son spilling out of me …

The doctor smeared cold ultrasound jelly over my swollen belly to find the rapid heartbeat of a child.

"Only one child miscarried," he said.

Simon the Parasite

Her light, it envelops you
As she carries you inside
Hiding you from the darkness
Protection from the callous
Passionately assisting
As you tug on the ribbon
Her sweet little parasite
The innocent blueberry
She changes her life for you
Because everything is clear
A dream state lucidity

Inside a beautiful mind
Her love, it embraces you
As she wonders who you are
Who you will turn out to be
She is scared, but so are you
It is inherently cruel
This place of hate called the world
But her love will embrace you
Healing hands, they will hold you
You'll smile as she shows you
All the beauty to be found

Scrub

It's a maze of endless hallways and all the doors are the same color except for mine. My door is painted red with the numbers 691 etched onto a little plaque above the keyhole. Ethan and I live on the sixth floor in the ninety-first flat. That's how the building works, with even numbered tenants living on the right and odd ones like me on the left. When I return from work, there's a folded piece of paper tucked beneath the door—smashed against the mat—with a copy of a copy of a copy of my lease agreement stapled to it: page three. There's a circled section of small print near the bottom for me to read.

As usual, our even-numbered neighbor awaits my arrival with a smile, his robe giving birth to a hairy beer gut. Even though he's old enough to be my father, the oily bastard doesn't mind undressing me with his eyes while I fetch the note.

The circled text reads: "Tenants shall not modify exterior walls and / or doors." The remaining scribbles tell me to return the door to its original color and provides a paint code I can take to any number of stores: 1325DS#2-66.

This isn't the first time I've come home to this type of notice, but until the stain's gone from my kitchen floor, the front door remains a vibrant, reminding red.

"Can I help you?"

"You a scrub nurse?"

I want to tell him *No, the blue scrubs are a fashion statement,* but I politely nod instead.

The man grins. Only one side of his mouth moves, as if he'd survived a stroke. He scratches himself, turns away, and enters his studio. The building was a hotel at one time, later converted to cheap housing; so his flat's down the hall a bit, across from ours. For two months I've put up with him standing there, waiting for me when I come home from work. He asks a different question every day that doesn't need answering.

After heating up a microwave dinner and forcing half of it down, I go to the kitchen floor. It haunts me, calls to me each day more than the last. The kitchen is where he died. Gunshot wound to the head. I find a new brush under the sink—the bristles on the old one are nearly gone—and instantly go to work on removing my husband's death from the cold linoleum.

As I scrub, I see it clearly: Ethan's corpse gazing at the ceiling, a blackish-red hole above his right eyebrow, a pool of blood surrounding his head. The granite countertop and the blender and the toaster and dishes in the sink—even the faucet handle. I cleaned the blood spray from all of it after he was taken out, but the blood on the floor remains a stain.

It lifts a little more each day.

Our neighbor should ask: "Why don't you move on?"

Not until Ethan's gone, I would say.

I clean until the brush is a light shade of pink and frayed, and then I go out to get the paint.

My job is what keeps me sane following Ethan's murder. During the day, I wear the rubber gloves, the facemask, the fancy blue hairnet, the matching uniform. Everything I do in life involves organization and cleaning messes, it seems.

I come home to the same jerk waiting outside his studio.

My door is still red.

No note this time.

No stupid question.

He wants *me* to ask the question this time, but I don't.

The next day, he's there. He wears a wife-beater and a pair of jeans with a belt trying to bury itself in the giant chasm of his belly button.

"Got another notice," he says.

It's wedged under my door and I ask if he put it there.

He sips his can of cheap beer with that stupid-looking smile.

"Want me to paint your door?" he says. "I don't mind doing it for you."

It sounds sincere, but I'd then owe *him* a favor.

"Please don't paint my door. Stay away from my apartment."

"Just being nice."

"Thank you, but no thank you."

He stands there as I pick up the note. It's the same message as before—the same copy of a copy of a copy of page three from our lease agreement. Ethan's name is still listed as the primary resident, I notice, as well as the circled small print near the bottom about tenants not modifying exterior walls and / or doors. The scribble tells me to return the door to its original color, like before, and provides a different paint code: 451MA-48.

I skip dinner this time and work on the kitchen floor before going out to get the paint.

"Another notice?"

It's another one of his questions that doesn't need answering.

"Please, I don't need this right now."

We lost a patient in the ER, so my day isn't off to a great start. It was an extensive operation involving two surgeons and took most of the day. I was in charge of draping and gloving the team, blood irrigation and monitoring blood loss for the patient, as well as counting needles, sponges and sterilizing instruments.

A really long day.

"I asked you to stay away from my apartment."

He points to his door, fewer than ten feet away.

"Don't you get tired of seeing them under your door?" he says.

I do. I come home to a red door each day and am reminded of Ethan. I want to paint over the red and move on. Instead, I come home to my red door, the same note, the codes.

The paint codes are really just that: codes.

1325DS#2-66 stands for 1325 D Street, Apt. 2. The number 66 tacked onto the end of it is simply the last two digits of the zip code. Not rocket science. The second address of 451MA-48 translates to 451 Morris Avenue, a different part of the city.

My neighbor wants me to talk.

I don't want to. I don't want to talk about the lease agreement and the fake message about painting the door. I want to go inside and scrub. I want to forget that Ethan died because I once received a notice wedged under my door with a paint code of 101FR#691-70. This one stood for 101 Feagleship Road, Studio 691: our studio apartment.

I put a bullet through Ethan's head.

It was a lot of money.

The blood stain on the kitchen floor calls for me.

Soon I'll be able to paint the door and move on, but not until Ethan's gone.

I sign for an overnighted FedEx box that contains fifteen thousand in unmarked, messy bills to cover the last two jobs. The package is an Amazon box with a return address of someplace a thousand miles away. I'm not even sure where the money comes from, only that it's never late, and is laundered and shipped from phony company called ABC Books. Books hide the money well. Inside I find a stack of hollowed bibles, the pages cut out to make room for the cash. Sometimes they're bibles. Sometimes they're encyclopedias. On a Post-it stuck to the inside of the first book is a name to verify against the next coded address: JAMES PILCHEN.

The Internet gives me directions to his house and his Facebook profile is public. He lives seven miles away and I've seen his face. That's all I need—or want—to know about him.

I twist the silencer onto the barrel of my Colt .38 and

check the chamber before sliding it into my concealment holster.

My neighbor doesn't greet me when I leave. In less than fifteen minutes my car is parked half a block down from the decoded address for James Pilchen. Surgical gloves wait for me in the glove box. Ten grand for this guy.

I sit in the car reading a *Repairman Jack* novel on my Kindle and lower the digital book every few pages over the course of several hours. He has a yapping dog in the living room that yaps even louder when a black Mercedes pulls up the driveway. He's got a wife, a trunk full of groceries, a little girl in a paisley dress.

Ethan wanted kids.

I drink at a bar called *The Stagger Inn* until I shouldn't drive, and then I stagger out.

A text message on my phone from several hours ago reads *When you're out, you're out*

—from an unlisted number.

It can only mean one thing.

I should be arrested for driving while intoxicated, or should have at least crashed along the way, but manage to turn onto Feagleship Road and make it home in one piece.

The maze of endless hallways smells like paint and my door matches all the others in the apartment. Even over the alcohol, I can smell it. The door is painted eggshell white with the numbers 691 etched onto a little plaque above the keyhole. A folded piece of paper waits for me, tucked beneath the door—smashed against the mat—with a copy of a copy of a copy of my lease agreement stapled to it: page three. There's a circled section of small print near the bottom for me to read, but I already know what it says. I've read it a dozen times before. I'm only concerned with the paint code, which I've also seen before: 101FR#691-70.

My neighbor is not there to greet me. He has no more rhetorical questions for me to answer and is done sliding notes underneath my door.

Ethan's name is crossed out on the lease agreement. I go inside, but not to scrub, because he's gone. I go inside to paint the kitchen floor.

Ink

Scribbles on the paper
A page once white
The page is reddening
There are no words
No questions to answer
Nothing to write

Only deep lines
Jagged and crimson streaks
Ink running down
Bleeding until empty
The page is blank

The page is full of shit
Bleeding until it tears
Ink to forget
Cuts that won't disappear
Many deep lines

Nothing to say
No answers to question
There are some words
The page no longer white
A page turned gray
Scribbles on the paper

Eavesdropping

Tell the lady in the piss yellow blouse to put away her phone.

The elongated rearview mirror reflected the woman in yellow four seats back on the right side of the bus. She wore sunglasses that were too big for her face and made her look like a bug. She held a smart phone to her ear and yapped away, her voice unusually high-pitched. The woman across from her was eavesdropping, Ned could tell, though the term originally implied listening secretly to a private conversation—while standing on an eave, no less; this woman's conversation was anything but private. The seven other passengers seemed annoyed with her as well.

"Miss?" he said from the driver's seat, meeting her bug eyes in the mirror. The woman in piss yellow kept talking, but he had gotten her attention. "Please end your call. No one wants to hear of your sister's missed period, and I don't believe she'd care for you telling everyone on my bus." It was rude. It could work.

A passenger in back snickered.

Despite the dark glasses, Ned could sense her eyes rolling.

He pulled over at the next stop, hoping she'd get up from her seat and leave. She stayed put when the brakes finished whining and the accordion doors hissed open and a young man wearing a knockoff military jacket entered. He made his way to the second row from the back and sat directly in front of the man in the white baseball cap who had been there since the first stop.

This is how Ned knew his passengers—by gender and apparel. He had a few regulars on his morning route, but most changed daily.

Ned waited for the new passenger to find a seat before closing the doors and moving on.

"I'm on the way," said the lady in the glasses. "Yeah, like five more stops. This driver's a total asshole. Told me to *end* my call. I *know*, right?"

Everyone on the bus heard her. She made sure of that.

Tell her to get off at the next stop.

"Ma'am? Yes, you again."

"Oh great, what does he want now?" she said into her phone.

"Lincoln Street is the next stop. I'm going to have to ask you to leave."

"What?"

"You're getting off at the next stop."

"No, I am not," she said, and then to her phone, "He's trying to kick me off now for talking to you. Can you believe that?"

Stop the bus.

There was no place to pull over.

Stop!

Ned braked and the taxi tailgating him swerved and laid on the horn. A line of cars stacked behind him as more people honked. It was the middle of rush hour and Ned was a bus parked in the middle of the street.

"What the hell?" the man in the military jacket said. The bug lady looked at Ned in the mirror. She shook her head and mouthed the words: You've got to be kidding me.

The mirror: a means of looking at people without looking at them.

"Get off my bus," he said.

"I'm not going anywhere. Just do your job and drive."

Make her leave.

Ned rose from the driver's seat and pulled the lever to open the accordion doors. He pointed to them. Most of the passengers did not seem to mind the scene. Those commuting around him were a different story.

"What's your problem?" the bug lady asked.

"I asked you nicely to end your call and you continued to yammer. Even now, you have that phone to your ear like it's a growth."

Good.

"Are you hearing this?" she asked her phone, and the other passengers.

"Please leave now."

She shook her head and continued her conversation.

In five seconds, she dies.

"Get off my bus."

Five.

"I pay my taxes and my taxes pay your wages. Do us all a favor and keep driving the damn route. I'm not getting off 'til my stop."

Four.

"This is your stop."

Ned took a step toward her but she avoided looking at him.

Three.

"Ma'am, I'm warning you," he said, but there wasn't much he could do. He faced her in the mirror. "Listen to me and—"

Two.

"You're out of your mind. I'm not walking from here. You're a fuckin' lunatic."

"Please, lady!"

These wheels better roll.

His eyes moved to his own reflection, to the Bluetooth headset over his ear.

Ned closed the doors and took his foot off the brake.

One.

Ned pressed the pedal to the floor and the bus lurched forward. Buses were designed for mass transit, not dramatic acceleration. They were nearly flowing with traffic when the lady in the bug glasses dropped the phone, her face slamming hard into the headrest in front of her. He glanced long enough to see her crumple into the aisle.

"Oh my God!" said the man in the military jacket.

Ned's focus was the road, but he saw the man move toward her in his peripheral vision, then squat down beside her.

"She's bleeding."

She should have listened.

The voice: perched on his eave.

"Driver, stop the bus."

Drive.

"She's bleeding! Stop the bus. I think she's been shot."

Commotion amongst the passengers.

"She hasn't been shot," Ned told them.

The woman in the red blouse, another regular, blurred across the glass as she joined them in the aisle.

"Her ear," she said. "What's happened to her ear?"

"Call 911," someone suggested, probably the guy in the white baseball cap in the back.

"No!" Ned said, slamming the brakes.

Don't you dare *stop!*

"Driver, stop the bus," the man in the jacket repeated. "What the hell's your problem, man? Pull over. I'm calling the police."

Ned turned in his seat and their eyes met as the man pressed the phone to his head.

The woman in red screamed a few seconds later.

Ned looked to the mirror, to the dead woman with the bug glasses sprawled in the aisle. Now the man draped over her, clutching his own cell phone in a literal death grip. A stream of blood ran from his ear and onto the dead woman's face.

The woman in red shook him and screamed again. She ran to the front of the bus and banged against the doors. "Stop the bus!" Her hands smeared blood on the glass.

"I can't."

He thought of quickly yanking the wireless headset from his ear and throwing it aside, but the other deaths were so instantaneous that he couldn't afford the risk.

I know what you're thinking, and I wouldn't try it if I were you. See the car to your left, the silver Honda?

The driver was a young man with his hat turned sideways. His windows were down and beats coming from his stereo over-powered the engine noise of the bus. He held a cigarette or a joint in one hand and a cell phone in the other. He looked like he was singing to Ned—rocking to the music—and then his head fell back and the rest of him went limp.

Fading honks from the traffic they passed.

The woman up ahead Jaywalking …

—her knees buckled mid-stride and she fell, face smashing against the asphalt. Both her briefcase and cell phone fell with her.

The kid riding his bike on the sidewalk, staring at you and your bus …

—he was still pedaling when he collapsed over the handlebars and swerved over the curb. The bike fell into the street and Ned had to pull hard on the wheel to avoid running him over. The driver behind him wouldn't be so lucky.

"Stop this."

The woman in red ...

—she held a cell phone to her ear with her back against the glass and kept her eyes on Ned and dropped next to the accordion doors.

So many people, reliant on technology. So many inconsiderates, jabbering away. So many conversations, all at once.

"Why are you doing this?" Ned asked the man in the white hat at the back of the bus.

It had to be him.

He was the quiet one throughout all this.

Ned's headset crackled, distorting the broken answer.

"Why are you doing this?"

The man in the cap ignored him.

"You might as well kill me," Ned told him.

Ned accelerated and brought the bus up to fifty miles per hour. They had finally made it to less congested traffic where the posted speed limit was twenty-five.

"You hear me?"

Vehicles flew past in blurs. The bus reached sixty, then seventy. Pedestrians on the sidewalk pointed. Ned swerved the bus around a black sedan, clipping the fender.

The man in the back ignored him, closed his eyes and held onto the seat in front of him.

"I said you might as well kill me!" Ned said to his tiny body in the mirror.

Eighty as Ned swerved into his original lane and adjusted his headset.

The bus leaned.

"You hear me?"

Wheels hit curb.

"I'm the driver. I'm in control!"

Ned overcorrected and slammed into the side of a blur in the left lane. The bus bounced over and onto the curb momentarily. He pulled the wheel to regain control, wondering when he'd hear the frequency in his ear and fall over dead like the others, the call killing him. Pedestrians scattered, their screams silenced by the scraping metal, a bike disappearing under the bus, a woman running for her life but unable to save it as the side view mirror struck her head and spun her to the ground.

I'm in control, the voice repeated.

Passengers lay dead in the aisles of the bus; they lay dead in the streets.

He rammed into the back of a Volkswagen. The bus climbed over its bumper and through the rear window, smashing the fragile car into a crumpled mess as the bus spilled to its side. A glance to the elongated rearview mirror revealed the woman in the piss yellow blouse and the man in the military jacket—tossed like dolls—dancing in the aisle for a moment—alive for that moment, the original eaves-dropping woman in red crumpling against the accordion doors, and the man in the white baseball cap in back falling onto a set of windows now under him.

The bus scraped to a halt.

A frequency resonated as blood dripped from Ned's ear and onto the woman in red. He was strapped to his seat, arms dangling, the pitch in his ear rising. Everything side-ways as he waited to die. The passengers who were thrown about, the people in their cars and in the street and on the sidewalk, the little boy on the bike—the bastard in his ear had killed them all.

The man in the white baseball cap stood on broken windows and reached into his pocket, pulled out a cell.

"I'd like to report an accident," he said into it after dialing. "I don't know … A bus. The driver, he tried to kill us."

The voice—nothing like the one in his ear.

"No!"

It wasn't him.

No.

Ned unclipped his seatbelt and dropped three feet onto the woman smashed against the accordion doors.

The man in back finally acknowledged Ned, stared right at him in fright, crumpled to his knees and fell. Blood seeped from his head like the others. Dead.

"Don't use your phones!" Ned said to the remaining three passengers.

The buzz in his ear intensified as static behind it turned to words.

Don't use your phones! this voice repeated, but not from his headset, which had fallen off during the accident. He was no longer in conversation with whoever had called him. He was in conversation with himself.

"Don't use your—" he started.

Don't use your— the voice echoed, his own voice.

The deaths had nothing to do with cellphones.

A brunette woman in a gray pullover looked into his eyes, fell over dead.

A girl of about seven crawled out from the mess around her and their eyes met.

"No," he said, but it was too late to turn away.

No, his own voice resonated as she collapsed.

He had killed them with his eyes; every last passenger but one.

Ned tried to look away, to not look at him with his deathly vision, but the only person still alive in the bus put a hand on Ned's shoulder and he instinctively turned. The Good Samaritan smiled as he died—an awful sound as his head connected with something metallic.

Accident gawkers gathered around the bus.

Ned heard them shouting. He listened to their panic as they experienced the wake of destruction he had caused on the streets and sidewalk. Voices everywhere. Shouting. Dozens of conversations.

So many people, jabbering away.

He eavesdropped on them all.

The elongated rearview mirror was now vertical and reflected Ned's upper half. He avoided his mirrored self, but knew there was only one way to stop the killer.

Blood continued to run from his ear.

Someone had jumped on top of the bus and was banging against the windows. When the noise stopped, Ned imagined a person cupping his hands against the glass, peering inside. If he could see Ned, he'd see a man staring at himself in the mirror, willing himself to die.

"I'm going to kill you," Ned told his reflection.

He waited for the voice in his head to say the same, yet heard only the conversations of others trying to get inside.

Listen to Me

I know what's good for you
I know what you should need
I know what push you like
I know what makes you bleed
Listen to me
Listen to me
Listen to me!

I hear all your thinking
I hear all your prayers
I hear all your beliefs
I hear all your layers
Listen to me
Listen to me
Listen to me!

I take what is evil
I take what gives you pain
I take what brings sadness
I take what you refrain
Listen to me
Listen to me
Listen to me!

I forgive all your wants
I forgive all your cries
I forgive all your debts
I forgive all your lies
Listen to me
Listen to me
Listen to—

It Tears Away

He pulls the triangle flap on the top of his thigh and it starts to crawl out of him, the thing living underneath responsible for killing John Parkinson. It's part liquid—this warm after-birth—and runs down his leg as he tears at the layers to get to Ward Phillips.

Why did you do it? Why did you kill him?

There is no laughter, but he can sense the sarcasm.

I didn't kill anyone, Ward tells the enveloping black.

Solitary confinement. The box. His third day.

The thing crawling out from under his skin knows the secret. The shell of the man trapping Ward had nothing to do with the death of John Parkinson or any of the others.

He was in prison for tax evasion and embezzlement; he wasn't responsible for the bad things.

You had me sharpen a spoon by rubbing it against the floor of our cell. I slid it across John's throat while he slept, but we both know that wasn't me behind the wheel.

That wasn't death you gave him, says Ward.

We murdered him.

That was rebirth.

He was our cellmate and he is dead, which is why we are in this sarcophagus. He was a good man, someone sorry for the sins he committed, someone paying his dues. He was getting out of here in six months and now he's—

And now he's home.

Another layer lies beneath, yet so much traps the one inside. The skin stops peeling and when he gives it a tug, it rips free. The thought crosses his mind to devour the nasty thing, to let his body digest and destroy the chassis. He instead drops it by the other pieces and starts over again, digging into the soft skin on the inside of his bicep. Fingers rake across his body over and over again.

Why are you hurting yourself?

To let you free, Ward.

Why?

The family of four in Calsbury. You broke into their home and stabbed the father in the heart and the mother when she woke, killed both their children while they were sleeping, propped the entire family upright on the couch in their living room on blood-soaked cushions until the early hours of morning, taped their eyes open so they'd watch the bad things ... the schoolgirl in Brenden you kept from screaming by stuffing her throat until her body stopped resisting and then tossing her into the bushes ... the young mother with the tattoos and her unborn—

I saved them all.

When authorities showed us the crime scene photos, you turned away. You wouldn't look at them, but I had to. There is no saving for someone like you. You are a monster. A destroyer of worlds. And now you're in a box like me and need out. I'm helping you escape this prison, Ward. All this black you see around you—that's your freedom, a taste of purgatory. I'm letting you out so you can see what your Hell will be like, so you can see—

There is nothing to see. My eyes are closed.

The man in solitary claws at his eyelids and tears them away so that Ward underneath has no other option than to forever see when the doors to solitary finally open.

Your eyes are the gateway, Ward. You can never close them again.

The man is slippery; it's difficult to pierce the skin, his fingers sliding in the syrup. The pain should be overwhelming, but he had stopped caring after the second day in solitary.

Pain, a simple reminder of purpose. A penance.

When they let us out of here, I will be all but gone. They will see that you are nothing like me. You will be reborn and they will see what kind of monster is underneath all this.

What if I want out—

Don't worry, you'll get out.

—of you? What if I am the reason you are doing this, controlling your body so that I have a means of finding this black 'freedom' you think is so … unfortunate? Have you thought about that? Do you think John Parkinson was a mistake, that I regret staring through your eyes as you straddled him on the cot and sliced open his neck, that I wasn't laughing inside—my body within your body—as they discovered you in our cell with that flabbergasted look on your face after you realized what you were doing?

Salty copper enters his mouth as he bites the back of his hand. He pulls until a chunk comes free. Hot liquid Ward gushes down his throat and the back of his hand pulses as more of him escapes. The room—so small—is suddenly smaller, the walls closer. His elbows and knees scrape against the inside walls of what had been coined 'the box' by fellow inmates.

The place they put the *really* bad people.

I can control this.

Footsteps approach as he shreds his cheeks. With no room left underneath the fingernails, his face grates like a block of cheddar. He breaks the strings dangling from his chin and goes at it again and again until his face is skinless.

Outside the box, two men—unaware of his transformation—converse in muffled voices; inside the box, the man housing Ward Phillips finishes removing the shell.

I am almost free.

Someone laughs and pounds outside the container ... his coffin.

His feet slide. The air is thin.

You are almost free.

Handfuls of hair are yanked from his head. He peels the scalp, wet dreadlocks of matted hair between his fingers.

I didn't kill anyone, he tells the white as the door opens.

There are no more layers.

Ward had everything to do with the death of John Parkinson and all the others. He was responsible for the bad things.

This isn't death I'm giving you, he tells Ward.

I murdered them.

This is rebirth.

And now you're home.

All but the Things that Cannot Be Torn

Underneath violet
A violent unrest
Resentful commands his
Hands dance so hesitant
Hastened pulls to sunder
Over pools underfoot
Feats not worth regretting
Forgetting vile layers
Veiled white sheets of onion
A union of tastelessness
Lest the wasteful contempt
Tempting pain as it rips
Away a grip so strong

Along the line he peels
Feeling warmth and trickles
Tickling tendons beneath
Neither torment nor ache
For a fake set of ties
And he tires and stops
Horrid flops on the floor
More broken and soaking
Forsaken pieces of
A sad dripping man with
No plans or ways out from
This weight on his shoulders
It smolders conditioned

Contradicting comfort
Comes fortunes of anguish
Angered masquerades of
Masses raiding the torn
Tearing eyes and cursing
Nursing the denial
And undeniable
Dismay the dead see as
A purgatory sea
Purged stories so bloody
Muddy red to be sought
With thoughts all forgotten
Of the rotten tossed skin

The Dying Gaul

Oh! let that eye, which, wild as the Gazelle's
Now brightly bold or beautifully shy,
Wins as it wanders, dazzles where it dwells,
Glance o'er this page, nor to my verse deny
That smile for which my breast might vainly sigh
Could I to thee be ever more than friend:
This much, dear maid, accord; nor question why
To one so young my strain I would commend,
But bid me with my wreath one matchless lily blend.

Such is thy name with this my verse entwined;
And long as kinder eyes a look shall cast
On Harold's page, Ianthe's here enshrined
Shall thus be first beheld, forgotten last:
My days once number'd, should this homage past
Attract thy fairy fingers near the lyre
Of him who hail'd thee loveliest, as thou wast,
Such is the most my memory may desire;
Though more than Hope can claim, could Friendship less require?

– Childe Harold's Pilgrimage (To Ianthe)

On woolen sheets we lie, vulnerable and as white and bare as the stars against the black marble sky, placed by the hands of love gods in a triangle of three.

Ianthe: I cannot have her; she belongs to another in marriage. Her wondrous beauty—she is on her back—stares upside-down at a set of rotten eyes that capture and hold her own as she is penetrated, moaning her fake moans, the tears welling on her cheeks from both pleasure and pain, while her quavering body creaks the bed underneath. A head is mounted high on the wall, held by an iron stake: a fallen barbarian whom her husband Cadmon had slain with much contempt—a worthy foe. The pegged part of this dead man watches as Cadmon exits the luscious gap between her legs. He tosses her aside like spoiled meat and I, just a boy, reach for the silk flesh below her navel; but my wrist is taken and held at my back as he flips me around and pilfers me next, the fingers of my other hand only capable of caressing her thigh before they are guided away. Ianthe takes herself in one hand and her breast in the other. She cries out to the man on the wall and the sound is angels with clipped wings falling from heaven.

She is twice my age and I have known her half my life. Harold, my sweet, she calls me. She is my love, but I cannot have her; I can only be had for now, she tells me when we are alone. I am not yet of age, but I see the way she looks at me when the three of us are together or even when we are not. Her smile holds a secret. Her body smells of lust. Her touch is desirous, but cautious. We can never be together without Cadmon, she says, for I am not yet a man.

Someday I will join the battle and become a greater warrior than Cadmon could ever be. Someday he will die in melee and I will take his place inside my love. I will take her from the back, from the front, from the side, and she will cry out; but only because it pleases her and because it is me and not her joyless husband. There will be no pain as her body swallows my seed to bear a child. She will whisper my name: Harold. Together, we will melt.

For he through Sin's long labyrinth had run,
Nor made atonement when he did amiss,
Had sigh'd to many though he loved but one,
And that loved one, alas! could n'er be his.
Ah, happy she! to 'scape from him whose kiss
Had been pollution unto aught so chaste;
Who soon had left her charms for vulgar bliss,
And spoil'd her goodly lands to gild his waste,
Nor calm domestic peace had ever deign'd to taste.

And now Childe Harold was sore sick at heart,
And from his fellow bacchanals would flee;
'Tis said, at times the sullen tear would start,
But Pride congeal'd the drop within his eye:
Apart he stalk'd in joyless reverie,
And from his native land resolved to go,
And visit scorching climes beyond the sea;
With pleasure drugg'd, he almost long'd for woe,
And e'en for change of scene would seek the shades below.

– Childe Harold's Pilgrimage (from Canto the First)

I spy her through a silken shade. Ianthe dresses with patience and dignity, the white fabric draping over her shoulders and down like an ocean wave sprayed against the upper shore of her bosom. Her long brown hair is in braids; it falls between the valleys of her back. Her bare feet on the floor bend against the cold and her toes dimple. Gold rings jangle from her ankles as she shifts balance and places more jewelry on the soft lobes of her ears. She looks back and sees my stare. I blush and so does she. A smile forms from the edge of her carved mouth as she turns back to her husband.

I see the red spider webs stretching between the yellow of Cadmon's eyes as I part the shade that separates us. I heard his stupefied drinking the night before as I lay in bed thinking of nothing but Ianthe and that sweet caress of her thigh. They argued through the night.

Cadmon does not see me just yet. He sees the crescent smile on his wife's face.

He brings the backside of his hand across her mouth and the smile is gone as quickly as it formed. He stands a full foot taller and towers over her, his face flushed. He wears only a torc around his neck. His giant triangular chest reveals a pair of sweaty breasts larger than those of my love, strewn with criss-crossed battle scars. Bulging abdominal muscles mock his flaccid manhood; it hangs below them like the husk of a shriveled reptile. He stands before her, a giant with a wrinkled date wedged between his legs.

I desire nothing more than to see his head nailed above the bed one day as Ianthe takes me in as her own. To see her struck fills my heart with a wrath that burns and rises within my throat. There is nothing I can do but swallow it back down, for Cadmon is three times my size and he would take my life. He could easily crush my throat with a single hand.

A tear falls from her cheek. One falls from my own.

Ianthe holds her head and sobs as Cadmon leaves her. He takes his sword from the wall and walks naked out into the cool morning air. He must train for battle. The tip of the sword scrapes across the floor.

As I part the silken shade further, I wait eagerly for the sound to disappear, signaling Cadmon's absence.

I quietly rush to her aid.

She is bent in half, clutching her face.

I pull a delicate hand away from her swollen jaw. Her lip is split and leaking red. She doesn't want me to see her cry. Her hand pulls back, but mine is stronger. I tell her I love her, but she pushes me away. She tells me to leave—that we can never be together, or it would mean the death of us both—but I stay at her side.

She shakes as I wipe the blood from her mouth and lift her head so she looks directly at me. I kiss the wound, my eyes never leaving hers. I taste her blood on my lips.

Ianthe kisses me back and touches my tongue with her own. She quakes, as do I. Her sputtering breath is warm and smells like ripened peaches. She takes my palm from her cheek and this time she is stronger. She flattens my hand under her own and guides it down the soft skin of her neck, her chest, and underneath the fabric of her gown. The curve of her left breast leads to a mound of blissful heaven. The god at its peak trembles between my fingers. Her other hand finds a forbidden part of me.

Cold steel and sick warmth ends our connection. Cadmon separates me from Ianthe with his sword. He pushes me back and the edge digs into my flesh. The blade at my neck, I only come to his chest. Eyes bulge, as do dark veins on his brow. He breathes fast and raspy and I taste the hot drink on his breath. He looks down at me, ready to add my head to his collection.

My head is not worth your efforts, I tell him, but he doesn't listen. He has taken many lives and many heads, all worthy opponents. I am nothing to him but a tighter hole of pleasure.

Ianthe cries out.

Cadmon turns.

Spare his life, she pleads.

Cadmon twists back to me, ready to slice the blade through my neck.

I close my eyes, ready to die, my last thoughts of Ianthe and our encounter, her soft skin against mine, her eyes to mine, her lips to mine. Her breast under my fingertips. I imagine for a moment my head nailed above their bed—our bed—watching her beauty forever.

Cadmon leans into me.

Banish him! She shouts and I open my eyes in horror.

Kill me, I say, unable to grasp the thought of exile.

He pulls the blade away.

Tears run the course of my cheeks as I look at Ianthe. She stares at the ground before her and moves her hands to her gown. She loosens the straps and lets the fabric fall from her shoulders to the floor, leaving us with her nakedness.

The sight of her saddens me more. In all her goddess beauty, it is the swelling purple of her cheek that draws my attention. I look at Cadmon's sword, but would try at my own life before attempting to take his.

Again he raises the blade. For an instant, I feel there is

hope. But instead of dismembering my head, he uses the handle to strike me down.

The sun, the soil, but not the slave, the same;
Unchanged in all except its foreign lord—
Preserves alike its bounds and boundless fame
The Battlefield, where Persia's victim horde
First bow'd beneath the brunt of Hellas' sword,
As on the morn to distant Glory dear
When Marathon became a magic word;
Which utter'd, to the hearer's eye appear
The camp, the host, the fight, the conqueror's career,

The flying Mede, his shaftless broken bow;
The fiery Greek, his red pursuing spear;
Mountains above, Earth's, Ocean's plain below;
Death in the front, Destruction in the rear!
Such was the scene—what now remaineth here?
What sacred trophy marks the hallow'd ground,
Recording Freedom's smile and Asia's tear?
The rifled urn, the violated mound,
The dust thy courser's hoof, rude stranger! Spurns around.

– Childe Harold's Pilgrimage (from Canto the Second)

A ship awaits my departure, but I look back to it with baneful eye. It is there to lead me to foreign lands, away from what most I desire. The hilltop provides an awful view of the flat blue sea to my back, the ship nothing more than a brown crumb dropped into the water. At my front is a battle. Perhaps Cadmon will die this time, which would nullify my expulsion from this land. I could lie with Ianthe and we would need not worry about hiding our love. As I sit clutching my knees to my chest, I hold a pile of rain-soaked soil and wonder how much blood has spilt on this land I have called home for the thirteen years of my life.

I remember running up these hills as a child and rolling down them on my sides. I remember the laughter, and it pains me to bring it all back; but I must, for it now amounts to nothing more than fallen memories as it passes through my fingertips.

A gray cloud looms over the battlefield, casting everything underneath in heavy shadow. The wind whirls cold.

A crow lands near my feet and tilts its head to look at me with a beady black eye. I toss some dirt at it and the bird flutters.

Watch, it says as it dances. It shakes the earth off its wings and turns its neck toward the battle. It looks back to me and caws.

Watch.

Watch what? I ask, and I know then it is Morrigan.

The crow doesn't answer. It only looks at me with a crooked head and what I assume are distrustful black eyes.

The two sides of war below grow eager as they wait for the horn. From my seat they are nothing but riled ants merged together, angered and ready to attack the opposing threat.

Listen, says the crow, as if it were she starting the battle.

For a moment, there is nothing but silence. Both sides below take a shared breath. I listen as a distant horn croons death. And then a thunderous roar erupts from the crowd and I wonder if it is only thunder from the clouds reigning over them. Soon these separate armies merge as one, as shield and sword create a cacophony of music from a symphony comprised of metallic and wooden instruments.

The harmony of life taking death, says Morrigan.

The crow dances once again, wings fluttering.

The music is for her.

Drums pound. Cymbals crash.

The crowd below dances with her. Most fall.

If only he would die, I tell the crow.

Morrigan says, I guard your death, but nothing more.

As the sun moves directly overhead, it passes through a hole in the clouds, removing the battlefield from shade. It reveals a field of red as her music dies down.

Only the soft moan of fallen men remains. One side has won, but only a handful basks in the glory—if it can be called such a thing. Those clinging to life are either left for dead, or pierced one last time with a blade by the victor.

Morrigan flies to the finished battle.

Cawing, she urges me to follow.

She leads me to the dead.

I walk through a maze of fallen barbarians, naked and covered in the life that once filled their hearts. They stare at me with hollow eyes. A hand missing its two smallest fingers grabs my leg before falling limp at my feet. I step over a twitching man, a blade pierced through his throat. He gurgles blood and finally stills.

Morrigan tells me to retrieve a blade.

I choose a dagger and pull it from someone's back. I pass once glorious men now missing appendages. Those that cling to life, I ease to death, for that is what she tells me to do. I approach two nude men clutched together tightly, arms wrapped around one another and moving as if making love; I realize it is simply one man fallen over another, the end of a spear poking through the lovers, binding the two in an eternal embrace. I cut each of their throats.

I cannot save them all, I tell her.

Our journey ends at a large granite stone, and Cadmon leans against its base. One hand braces his body upright; the other rests on his thigh. He is alone, and naked except for the crimson torc around his neck—exactly as I remember him from earlier that morning. He looks to the ground. At first he appears untouched, only fatigued from war.

Morrigan perches atop the rock. She urges me closer. Cadmon looks to me with shame and I notice his heavy panting and dripping torc. Blood surrounds his body and he seems to float buoyantly within it like the ship at sea set to take me away. His manhood lay on the ground beside him. Someone has cut it off, and it is that flaccid member and the attached flaps of skin clinging to it which hold his gaze. He bleeds from a hole between his legs; the blood pulses out of him.

The black crow on the rock laughs as Cadmon's body slowly drains. I wait for him to die before taking off his head with my dagger.

> *I see before me the Gladiator lie:*
> *He leans upon his hand—his manly brow*
> *Consents to death, but conquers agony,*
> *And his droop'd head sinks gradually low—*

And through his side the last drops, ebbing slow
From the red gash, fall heavy, one by one,
Like the first of a thunder-shower; and now
The arena swims around him—he is gone,
Ere ceased the inhuman shout which hail'd the wretch who won.

He heard it, but he heeded not—his eyes
Were with his heart, and that was far away;
He reck'd not of the life he lost nor prize,
But where his rude hut by the Danube lay,
There where his young barbarians all at play,
There was their Dacian mother—he, their sire,
Butcher'd to make a Roman holiday—
All this rush'd with his blood—Shall he expire
And unavenged? Arise! ye Goths, and glut your ire!

– Childe Harold's Pilgrimage (from Canto the Fourth)

I carry Cadmon's head with pride. It hangs at my side—now all but drained—as I think of Ianthe and how it has come to pass that we can be together as I had once dreamed. Cadmon watches the ship at sea as his head swings back and forth in pendulum. The vessel sails away without me aboard and his dead eyes cannot look away.

Those I pass glance strangely, for they recognize Cadmon and his sad fate. Is it respect, curiosity, fear?

It matters not. I swing his severed head by a wad of matted brown hair as one would swing a basket of fruits.

It is my gift to Ianthe.

And she waits for me.

Watch, says the voice of the crow.

I look around. The black bird is nowhere to be found.

The phantom word is only in my head; it sends cold water down my spine as I walk toward my love.

I see her through the silken shade.

On woolen sheets she lies naked, vulnerable, and as white and bare as the early evening stars forming in the sky.

She is the essence of beauty, and the outlined curves of her slender body remind me that our love will no longer be a triangle of three.

We can now be two as we form into one.

She will take me inside.

She will moan and call out my name.

Harold, she will whisper into my ear, and Ianthe, I will mutter in broken breath. Her back will arc skyward with pleasure. We will melt like wax from two candles placed close together. Tears will run down our cheeks.

Ianthe: I can finally have her; she belongs to no one. She is mine, I am hers. I raise the head as I enter the room.

But the smile on her face holds a secret, and her eyes cannot see what I offer.

The handle of a dagger protrudes from the soft flesh beneath her navel. Dead hands grip the hilt. She has taken her life.

I replace the head staked to the wall with that of Cadmon's. He looks upon us as I weep over Ianthe and slide the blade from her stomach. I toss it aside as easily as Cadmon had tossed Ianthe the night before. I kiss her cold lips. She kisses back. I confess my love, and this time fear doesn't cause her to push me away.

Cadmon watches with cloudy eyes.

Twisted

Waking up twisted
a mess made of sheets
eyes opening wide
hazel seeking blue
revealing the love
that holds together
and which pulls us close
as our hearts flutter

beating rhythmically
butterflies frantic
and then we smile
I see into you
you see into me
our lips connecting
with nothing to hide
it's heavenly sweet

The Mascot

Why did the mascot cross the road?

We were not drunk, let that much be clear. Leslie had a few too many drinks, but she rode shotgun and counted sheep when our RAM plowed into the sucker—a horrendous sound as red painted the hood and something large smashed into the windshield and rolled over us. Both headlights blew, the dark highway enveloping the truck in a moment. If truth be told, the man in the rabbit suit had leapt.

Let it be repeated: we were not drunk.

This really happened.

Leslie woke, of course, screaming, "What the hell, Greg!" and looked around the cabin, confused, terrified, trying to see through drunken eyes and smears of blood over spider web glass; *thunk-thunk, thunk-thunk, thunk-thunk* before she reached over and turned off the wipers.

"We hit something."

"No kidding," she said.

The truck slowed, slid in the shoulder gravel, stopped, and we stepped out into the black. Stars speckled the sky, clearly visible over the lightless highway. A crescent moon smiled upon us, as if it understood the answer to the joke.

For us to run him over, the moon would say.

We were a good thirty miles from any form of civilization and hadn't passed another vehicle in over an hour. Taillights lit the asphalt behind us red and in the distance lay a hazy silhouette of a crumpled man.

"A deer?" Leslie asked.

"Larger than a deer."

"Tell me it was an animal. Tell me we didn't just murder someone."

"We didn't murder anyone, Les. The bastard jumped into us."

"Jumped?"

"Hopped, really."

Leslie circled the truck and held a hand over her mouth when she saw the gore. Blood splattered the entire front end of the vehicle and smeared across the hood. Shreds of rabbit suit and flesh clung to the chrome grill. A meaty rib protruded from the radiator as steam vented. The man must have split apart like a water balloon, splashing everywhere.

"I told you it was a deer," Leslie said, pointing to an antler lodged into the other broken headlight.

It wasn't a deer; it was a man in a fucking Jackalope suit, and he had hopped across the road. He had turned his head before we struck him, and he had smiled.

The cellphone couldn't find a signal as we walked to the lump in the road, but it worked as a light source, creating a wedge of white to lead the way.

"Oh God," Leslie said, retching once before doubling over to puke.

The dead man remained smiling, his head twisted toward us while his body and limbs faced the opposite direction. One incredibly long bunny ear pointed up; the other soaked the fluid leaking from his cracked temple. He even had a fluffy white tail. A single antler stuck outward from his head; the other broken off—the one Leslie had tried prying out of the headlight. He wore one of those sticker nametags, but the words were smudged and looked Latin: *lepus temperamentalus*. The bunny suit had either unzipped or ripped open in the back, which was now the man's front, and inside he was naked.

"He's not wearing any clothes, Les."

She squatted on the ground near the fence that lined the highway, staring into the field, far enough away so that she was just another shape in the night.

"What are you doing out here, dressed like this?"

The dead man's eyes reflected the light of the cellphone.

Still no signal, which meant we either had to find help, or help had to find us. Both directions showed no signs of life.

We stared at each other for a good while before Leslie joined us and closed his eyes for him.

"Jesus, Greg. Have some respect. The man's dead. Look at him—well, don't look at him—but don't gawk at him like that either. Have you called the police?"

"No signal."

She took the cell phone and tried herself, handed it back.

"What are we supposed to do? We can't leave him here on the side of the highway like road kill."

We both stood in silence, waiting for answers, waiting for headlights.

"Is that a nametag?"

"Yeah."

"Did you find a wallet, a cell phone? Maybe he has a cell with coverage out here."

"He's soup, Les. The only thing in that suit—"

"We need to do something, Greg!"

"We can bring him with us."

That quieted her. The thought of putting him into the truck bed was unsettling, to say the least. We'd either have to drag him thirty feet to the truck, or reverse the truck to him; either way, the process involved lifting.

"You can't be serious."

"What choice do we have?"

"Leave him here, report the accident, and return with the police."

Something rustled.

"What was that?" she said, turning to the field.

"Leslie, it's the middle of the night, we're out in the middle of nowhere, and there are about a dozen types of nocturnal animals roaming about."

It didn't seem to matter. She reacted to the smallest of sounds.

"Let's come back for him," she said, "with help. Let's get out of here."

"We at least need to get him out of the road."

She nodded, understanding the importance. The last thing this poor sicko needed was to be run over a second time. It was the last thing we needed. He was already as dead as dead can get, but not moving him on our part could result in a hundred bad outcomes: someone swerving out of the way to avoid the lump in the road and crashing into the ditch, or swerving head-on into another vehicle, or rolling over his body and the remaining antler puncturing a tire and sending them end over end.

This guy in the middle of the road was a deathtrap.

Someone else could die.

Since the man's legs were already facing the ditch, we each grabbed a leg and pulled, and it was like pulling … well, it was like pulling a large, bloodied animal across asphalt. He must have weighed two hundred pounds, and his fur created friction. His blood trail appeared black.

When Leslie fell onto her ass, it wasn't because she slipped or lost her hold. The man's leg had disconnected at the knee somewhere within the bunny suit. She dropped the limp appendage, bit her fist, and ran to the truck.

It was then the field livened.

Small crunches.

Field grass brushing aside.

Leslie screaming.

It proved difficult moving the man in the bunny suit alone, but soon he was in gravel and less likely to get run over a second time.

Something assailed Leslie in the truck.

The dead man smiled like the moon.

Leslie stopped screaming and held her throat. At first it looked as though she was holding back another retch, but as she staggered closer, trails of red escaped from between her grasp and a second creature the size of a cat jumped down from the passenger seat of the truck and scuttled into the field.

Small crunches.

Field grass brushing aside.

Leslie no longer screaming.

Lurching forward, she let go a moment and blood shot out of her neck and splotched the ground. Three wounds punctured her throat like bullet holes. Blood seeped out of her chest from six others, three on each side. Something sharp had punctured her stomach and breasts. Small claw or bite marks pitted her face. All this was revealed as she stepped closer to the cellphone light and collapsed flat onto her face. A shaky hand rose and fell limp.

Something stirred in the field behind her.

Beady eyes reflected like red pearls from what light the cellphone offered; first one set, then another, and another. Moving the phone back and forth revealed a dozen glowing eyes gathered together. They stared at Leslie as a pack, stared at both of us, ready to pounce. The sound of a hundred more. One approached, its clown-like mouth dabbed in blood lipstick. It touched noses with their mascot and the man's eyes opened. His smile widened.

The joke was on us.

Secret Smile

Why do rainbows frown
with their prismatic lips on the ground?

Exposed by the rain
painted by the sun

their smiles lie buried
not making a sound

Are they hiding something from us?

Coulrophobic

The triangle wedge of sponge spreads the face paint. You stare at me through the glass, blue eyes outlined in oversized cartoon white. And your grin, that evil glossy blood grin, stretches from ear to ear—literally—in ill-rounded proportions.

You are a clown.

Dobo, you call yourself. I've never figured that part out.

It doesn't mean anything, it's not short for anything, and it's not a mash of words. You say your name, and it's like your lips are puckering to apply lipstick, something a woman would do while peering into a compact. But you're not a woman, and you're not wearing lipstick. You are wearing face paint, a lot of it, and have a look on your fake-happy face that says you killed someone or did something bad or something worse—to a young girl, perhaps, or a boy wanting one of your multicolored bulbs that float above the colorful ribbons tethered to your wrist. You hand them out in the park to all the eager children, and you smile with your fake smile, your real lips making a flat line, mime-like, silent.

Come, child. Come play with Dobo.

You shaved your head in patches, and dyed what's left tangerine. Hair sprouts from your head like cubes of orange wheatgrass. Thirteen splotches of gelled hair poke out from your smooth scalp, one for each of the balloons you hand out to the excited children every day.

They look at you with innocence, these children. They want you to do something funny, something odd, something clownish. They want to smile and they want to laugh and they want to be kids.

Dobo the silly clown, they say, I want a green balloon, they say, or a pink one, they say, or maybe a purple or red one. Make me a puppy, they say; but the balloons you carry are not the kind for making animals, or whatever else their imaginations conjure. If you were to speak, you'd say, *"I could make you a balloon that looks like a balloon, wouldn't that be nice? Here you go, child,"* and you'd untie one from your wrist and pretend to shape a balloon out of the balloon and then you'd tie the ribbon around their wrist, and they'd laugh because of your silliness.

You stare at me through the glass and it makes me sick. Bad vibes. Old memories.

Come play with Dobo, you said to me that first time, tying a yellow balloon around my wrist. You pinched my nose and told me you took it, with your thumb squeezed between your index and middle fingers. I knew it was your thumb and not my nose because I could see the nail polish. You looked happy because that's how you painted yourself, your breath like mint and your face like wet clay. I wanted to be like you. I wanted to paint my face like a clown so I could make people laugh. I wanted to smile all the time because a painted smile never stops smiling even if you want it to.

You took my hand and then you took more. You turned me into something. I later learned that every clown has a

unique face. Not one is like another. Clown faces are regis-
tered in some kind of clown face registry and you get an
official clown identification card that looks like a driver's
license, but with a clown face instead of a normal face.
But I didn't want a different face then. I wanted *your* face. I
wanted to take it.

I remember looking around for Mom to tell her that I
wanted to be a clown when I grew up, but she was talking
to some guy she knew at the cotton candy stand. She was
twirling a finger through her hair and teetering on her heels.
He was swirling his hand in what looked like an overturned
washing machine or a dryer and it was coating the white
rolled-paper cone thing in fluffy pink sugar lint. The finger
in her hair was making a smaller version that she'd never eat.
I had a string of ride tickets in one hand and your hand in
the other. You took me past the food trailers and it smelled
like deep fried sugar and barbeque and eggrolls and other
food-on-a-stick. I looked over my shoulder and Mom was
walking in the other direction with her head jerking around
as she called out my name.

And then we walked faster, with carnies tempting older
kids with darts and balls or whatnot to break things for
prizes.

You stare at me through the glass.

I already played with you, I say.

You say your name silently to make your mouth pucker.

I don't want to play.

You do.

I can see it in your face as you apply thick black eyeliner
and draw grotesque eyelashes and a tear on your cheek like
a prisoner marking time. You fix the white in places where

red and blue have crossed over where they shouldn't have. You fix the smile. You pinch a foam nose over your real nose and your breathing is muffled. You look at the bag of balloons on the counter next to the spool of ribbon, and then back to me.

Our eyes are connected. Yours follow mine. It's as if we're playing a staring game and neither of us wants to lose.

Dobo, I say, and you mock me, your lips puckering. I lose the game and look away, but I win because you are no longer there.

Open Auras

Demon black, absorb
Devour the light
As it lifts from these rending ties

Soak through, muddied red
Devour the heart
As it screams from this vacuous mind

Burnt orange, melt down
Devour the soul
As it leaks from these waxing eyes

Wake, fading yellow
Devour the truth
As it falls from this tiring grind

Molded green, find peace
Devour the air
As it climbs from these weakened cries

Take in, loving blue
Devour the hurt
As it frees from this psychotic bind

Violet, pour out
Devour the self
As it pools from these open lies

Reflect, angel white
Devour the dark
As it steals from this reticent blind

Underwater Ferris Wheel

The lanky gentleman in the pinstriped suit and moth-eaten neck ruffle staggers forward. He holds a card for you to take:

COME RIDE THE UNDERWATER FERRIS WHEEL

There is a mixed scent of caramel corn, candied apples, corndogs and spilled beer as Cate waits her turn in line with her son. The trailer has a sign lit with small yellowing bulbs, which works cordially with the other food trailers to light up the otherwise dark path of sweets, meats, and deep-fried foods on sticks.

She lets go of Ian long enough to dig in her purse for money.

"Large cotton candy," she says to the man leaning over the counter.

"Stick or bagged?" He points to the prefilled plastic bags of rainbow clouds lining the inside of the trailer.

In back, a man wearing a hairnet spins pink silk onto a conical cone of white paper.

She takes in the smells of hot sugar and oil.

"Stick," Cate says, and adds corndogs to the order.

She turns to her son to see if he wants ketchup or mustard or both, but he's gone. The couple standing in his place look past her to the menu.

"Ian?"

She expects him at the ticket counter because he wanted more rides, not food, and he isn't there, nor is he wandering around the carny games across the promenade.

The others in line don't seem bothered that he's disappeared.

Cate holds a twenty-dollar bill instead of her son and is no longer hungry, her appetite for junk food replaced with a gut-wrenching fear of losing him. The man leaning through the window balances a pair of hefty golden corndogs in one hand, the other expecting money. She hands him the bill, forgetting she took the cotton candy.

"Ma'am?"

He holds her food, calling for her as she calls for Ian.

"Did you see a boy?" Cate asks the couple, hand at her waist. "This high, blond hair, red and white striped shirt?"

She knows Ian chose his outfit to match the tents he'd seen from the road when they were first setting up the carnival. He'd pestered her the entire week to go.

They shake their heads and take her place as she steps out of the line.

Hundreds fill the food court and labyrinth of walking paths.

"Ma'am?" the man calls again.

She no longer cares about the food or the money. She holds onto the cotton candy like a beacon, hoping Ian will see the pink light and come running from out of the darkness.

"One more ride after we eat something," Mom says.

She drags him through the crowd, making her own path. Behind them, Ian's wake is swallowed by kids able to ride the bigger rides by themselves, drunken men stumbling around and hanging off each other, yelling, beers sloshing over plastic cups (even though Ian knew they were supposed to drink at *The Beer Tree*), and other kids—Ian's age—being dragged around by their parents.

Music blasts from speakers hidden around the rides: heavy metal, pop, what the older kids at school call dub step, and then country. The music changes as rapidly as the scenery, fading in and out as they make their way from the rides to the food court.

Ian has enough tickets clenched in his fist for two rides, but his mom wants to go with him on the Ferris wheel after they eat and that will use up all ten that are left.

"One last ride," she says, meaning either the marvel of their day would soon end, or they'd be going to do the stupid adult stuff, like seeing the animals, or going to the building with all the paintings and quilts, or to the place where they judge fruits and vegetables and jarred stuff, which they could see any other day by going to the grocery store.

And they still hadn't played any games.

"Step up, son," says a man who isn't his father. He holds a softball that's supposed to be tossed into a tilted basket without bouncing out. "It's easy," he says, tossing it under-hand, and it is easy because it stays in the basket, and he wasn't even looking at it.

"You can win one of these to take home."

Stuffed animals bigger than real animals hang from their necks.

"Can we play games?"

"After we eat, maybe."

Maybe means no most times.

The man with unkempt hair and brownish teeth leans out of the booth. Three baskets are lined behind him, no one else playing his game.

"Free game for the boy," he says.

"Mom!"

"There are no free games," she says, pulling him along. The man puts his hand to his heart.

"Honest. One free toss."

"Please, Mom?"

"A gift from me to you," the man says. "No money, I promise. Let the boy win something to take home. One free throw."

They stop. A bright disc of moon shines above, illuminating the two figures and casting them into a small circular spotlight.

Ian already knows he wants the dragon. It's red and about two feet long and has a forked tongue hanging out of its mouth.

The man who wants him to win the stuffed animal is within what his mom warned was 'grabbing distance' and holding a yellow dimpled softball like they have in the batting cages. He tosses another behind his back, which spins in midair and lands in the basket.

"One," says his mom.

"There we go! Step up to the counter here, but don't lean over, and simply toss it in."

He throws another spinning ball and makes it in, and Ian thinks he might have it down. It takes some backspin and needs to brush the upper, back portion of the basket.

Ian takes the ball, tries to copy the technique. The throw looks similar, but the ball hits the bottom of the basket and comes shooting out.

"Good try! I think you almost have it down." He holds out another yellow ball. "One more go at it."

"That's how they work," his mom whispers to him. "See?"

"One more for the boy."

"No thank you," she says.

The man in the booth sets the ball on the counter. "Try it again. No gimmicks. I want to see the boy get one in. You can try it, too," he says, placing a ball in front of her as well.

This time his mom's the one smiling, but her teeth are much whiter. She hesitates and lets go of Ian's hand.

"One more," she says.

She picks up the ball and throws it underhand, but doesn't put any spin on it so it bounces back at her and she he has to pick it up off the ground.

"The boy's going to do it," the man says. "I have a good feeling about this one."

Ian takes his turn and concentrates. He needs to throw it like last time, but not as high. He lets it roll off the tips of his fingers softly and there's plenty of backspin. It hits the basket in the right spot and nearly rolls out, but remains inside.

"He's a natural," the man in the booth says, crouching down behind the counter.

Ian points to the dragon, but the man stands upright

with a goofy smile. His prize is a cheap metallic-looking pinwheel tacked to the end of a straw that matches his shirt.

"Ah, you want the dragon," he says. "You gotta work your way up to that one by trading up from the smaller prizes."

He hadn't noticed the various prize levels until now.

"That's how they work," his mom says.

You flip the card in your hand to find the other side black. The white side, with the message about the underwater Ferris wheel, contains only the invitation to ride it and nothing more. The lanky man in the pinstriped suit is gone. You took the card and read the words and sometime in between, the man resembling a makeup-less clown vanished into the crowd, his coattails consumed by kids holding balloon animals.

Cate wanders, but doesn't want to stray from the food court because Ian can't be far and isn't prone to exploring on his own. She nearly steps onto a lone ticket, remembering Ian's longing for one final ride, and retrieves it from the ground.

Like money in his wallet, Ian counts the red tear-off tickets to make sure there are still ten. He lets them accordion out, the last ticket lapping a puddle of a spilled soda. He holds his mom's hand as she drags him around. It would be much easier to count them if he had his other hand. He tugs and his mom tugs back to let him know she's in control and that counting won't be very easy.

He's not even hungry, but they pass through ever-changing music and laughing and cheering and the shrill of those flipping cages on the *Zipper*, kids screaming through the fast loop of the *Ring of Fire*—yellow and red bulbs flashing in circular patterns as the coaster cycles first clockwise, then counterclockwise—and the mesmerizing vertical array of green, white, and blue bars of light on the *Gravitron* as it spins like a flying saucer dreidel.

A tongue of tickets trails behind as he counts. He folds them, one onto the next, with the flip of his index finger and thumb. He gets to five when a Goth girl he recognizes from school bumps into his shoulder and jars them loose.

They stop at a paved path to let a medic golf cart pass, and that's when Ian notices what he thinks is a clown. He doesn't resemble the colorful clowns with the big feet and honking noses and painted faces, and he's not one of those clowns squeak-tying balloons into poodles and pirate swords in the park. This one's unremarkable, except for the scrunched doily thing around his neck. He looks like someone from an old black and white photograph, like the ones hanging on his grandma's wall: pictures of his grandparents' parents. He thinks of this because the man is not smiling—lips pressed in a flat line—like old people in old photographs, dressed in an old black suit.

And he stares, eyes not moving away.

The cart has suddenly vanished, the world no longer paused. A soft tug on his hand tells him they're moving again and Ian looks at his feet for only a moment because someone's stepped on his laces and he nearly stumbles. Looking back, the man is gone, the crowd alive in his place.

"You've never had cotton candy before, have you?"

Ian shakes his head no, although she doesn't see him.

"When I was your age, I loved cotton candy," she says over the noise. "Me and your father used to go to the Brendan Carnival every year when it was still around."

When Dad was still around.

She always started conversations this way, always talking about what they did as a couple before Dad died, before a non-drunk driver clipped his car and drove him off a cliff and into the ocean where he drowned.

"Your father always liked the candied apples. He had a sweet tooth. Sometimes we'd share the … I'm not sure what it was called, but it was multicolored popcorn in these little rectangular shapes wrapped in plastic; each clustered section of color was a different flavor, like orange or cherry or grape, kind of like caramel corn but different. I haven't had that in years."

The symphony of carnival noise dulls the closer they get to the food court, the lights brighter, and the stench of puke, beer, and cigarette smoke lingering, yet overpowered by Chinese food, barbeque, and deep-fried everything.

"Wait'll you try the corndogs. Your father used to love those."

Nine tickets. There are only nine.

"Mom, we need to get another ticket to ride the—"

"No rides until after we eat. Here, this one looks good."

They stop in front of a trailer lit up in yellow bulbs and the entire thing glows. One of the smaller bulbs in the word SNACKS is missing, like his tenth ticket.

You attempt to follow him, but he weaves in and out of the multitude of people as if gliding over ice: a glimpse of a coattail, a pinstriped leg, night-black hair. He is quickly absorbed into crowds of parents and children and ages in-between. The wind picks up and you drop the card, which flaps along the ground like a dead butterfly. It flips over and along the ground as easily as it flipped in your hand and you can read the words in a strobe-like flutter of black and white—the invitation for the ride.

Cate turns a boy around, but it's not Ian.

She calls his name again and then sees him standing in front of a game booth fifty feet away. Warmth flushes through her body as she remembers to breathe, the thought of losing Ian more than she can handle. Losing a husband is one thing, but losing their only son who resembles him so undeniably …

"Ian!" She wills her voice to reach him.

He turns then, but not in her direction, and her heart drops.

Running to him, she continues to call his name, jouncing shoulders against those in her path and nearly trampling people over entirely. A double baby stroller trips her and she falls and scrapes her knee, then rises and keeps going, somehow never losing grasp of the lone red ticket and the cotton candy she points to the sky. Ian passes in and out of view, as if projected against the throng of fairgoers from a spinning shadow lamp.

"Ian!"

One moment he's there, the next he's not.

A flash of silver and the pinwheel he no longer wants falls to the ground. A gangly man leans over to pick it up— one of the carnival folk, perhaps. He's the only immobile person in the multitude and wears a black pinstriped suit, as out of place in the dark as a dandelion in a bouquet of yellow roses. An aged neck ruffle strangles his throat and he smiles as she approaches.

He offers the pinwheel, but she only wants her son.

Cate looks around him frantically.

"Did you see the boy who dropped that?"

The silence tells her he's mute. He stares at her, expressionless, his face drained of both color and emotion.

"I'm looking for my son, Ian. He dropped this," she says, taking it from him, "and you just picked it up. Did you see where he went?"

He doesn't point, nor does he say anything. He simply takes his finger and spins the cheap toy on the stick and magically reveals a card from one of his shirtsleeves. The man stands there a moment before facing the ocean pier.

He tugs on his mom's hand, but she doesn't tug back to let him know she's still in control. Glancing up, Ian finds that he's not holding his mother's hand at all, but the hand of a tall man with long arms that dangle well past his knees. He can't remember ever letting go, but he must have, and somehow grabbed this man instead. Clammy fingers curl around his own. It's the man who isn't a clown—the old photograph man he saw before.

Ian jump-startles and the man lets go.

He isn't scary because he doesn't wear a fake face like

regular clowns who pretend to be happy or sad or sometimes mad. He has a normal face.

He hands Ian a card.

"Are you supposed to be a mime?"

The man doesn't say anything.

"I read a story once about a mime and he never said anything, either. He would pretend to be stuck in invisible boxes and climb ropes that weren't really there. But he wore makeup and had a white face and black lips like Charlie Chaplin. I don't know who that is, but my mom says he looked like Charlie Chaplin."

He shows Ian the rest of the cards, which are bound together with a rubber band. His dad used to do card tricks, so Ian knows what to do. He's supposed to take a card and look at it without showing and hand it back. Ian's card is a stained joker with worn edges and a crease down the middle. The joker wears a jester hat and rides a unicycle and looks drawn in scribbles of pen.

Before he hands it back, the man splays the cards before him, at least two dozen. They are all different. About half are standard playing cards of different makes, some old, some new. Mixed within are handmade cards like the joker, along with baseball cards, a library card, credit cards, and a few drivers licenses from different states.

Ian hands the card to him facedown and watches as it's shuffled into the deck over and over again, and in lots of different ways. The unsmiling *carny*—his mom would call him that—bends the cards like his dad used to, shuffles them flat in the air with his thumbs, and then reverses the cards in an arc to slide them in place—what his dad called 'the bridge.'

He hands the deck to Ian.

"I pick one?"

The man doesn't say anything.

Expecting his card to be on top because the back looks similar, Ian lifts a three of diamonds, which looks as though someone with shaky fingers drew the number with black crayon and then smudged three red diamonds on the card with lipstick. The one after it isn't his card either, but a jack of clubs. He flips over the next card with stats printed on the back and it's a rookie card for someone who used to play on a team called the Royals; over the player's face is a smiley face sticker with the eyes scratched out. The next card is a VISA. The next is a king of hearts from a standard Bicycle deck, followed by a five-dollar bill ripped in half with a spade drawn in Sharpie over the President's face, and then a seven of clubs, and then another hand-drawn card.

Confused, Ian hands the deck back to him.

The man wraps a rubber band around them and slides them into his suit pocket.

"What's the trick?"

The man holds out his hand, as if peddling for money.

That's how they work, his mom would say.

Three of the fingers curl until he's pointing at Ian's pinwheel.

As if on cue, a cool breeze spins the cheap metallic flower around, which Ian didn't want anyway; he had wanted the dragon but his mom didn't want to pay for more games, even though he would have given up food to pay for a few more tosses into the basket so he could win the bigger prize. Dad would have let them play. If Dad hadn't died, they would have had enough money to play more games *and* ride more rides and *really* have fun.

Ian gladly hands over the pinwheel. In the process, the man who looks sort of like a clown clumsily drops it as part of a gag and they both fetch for it on the ground. Lying next to the cheap toy is Ian's joker card, which the trickster silently places into his pocket with the others.

He pulls out another card, but this time it's not one of the strange playing cards; it's a business card with a black side that reflects the moon and a white side that absorbs its light. A trade for the pinwheel, it seems. Printed on the white side is an invitation.

You hand the carnival worker five red tickets and he lets you past the chain and through the gate. A set of aluminum steps leads to a grated path to the ten-story wheel. Every angle of metal is lit by long neon lights and flashing bulbs that cycle in hypnotic patterns. The cart awaits—the slightly rocking yellow one with the number eight on the side. You are alone for the ride as you were in line, the carnival empty. A mechanical click and the wheel moves. The world drops with the wind at your back. You elevate in reverse as the wheel rotates on a giant silver axle. Rods and lights and the other carts fall as you rise. At the peak, black water rises from the pier, and for a moment you float above it all, nothing but sky and water and the thin line between. The entire lit wheel is cast against the water, appearing as though there are riders beneath the placid surface revolving horizontally, perhaps looking up to you in the stars. You see your reflection on the water, and then you free-fall fly, arms stretched outward, the wind at your face. The water rising.

COME RIDE THE UNDERWATER FERRIS WHEEL

Cate reads the card a second time and when she looks up from it, the man in the pinstriped suit is gone, like her son.

"Ian!" she calls.

She parts through people on her way to the water's edge, which seems so far away. Why would he go to the pier? Somehow she knew he'd be there, and somehow the man with the moth-eaten neck ruffle knew. He was leading her to the—

Your father and I would always ride the Ferris wheel, she had told Ian in the car. That's where she'd find him. She couldn't stop talking about it on their way to the carnival. *It was always the last thing we did before going home*, she had said.

Running takes the air from her lungs and pierces her side, but she spots him gazing up in wonder at the base of the ride. She spins him around to find his eyes glossy and terrified.

"There's no underwater Ferris wheel," Ian tells the water.

There's only the reflection of the real Ferris wheel.

"The card's a lie."

He walks along the planks, peering over the side to the black water. If there *was* an underwater ride, he'd at least see some kind of glowing light from below.

One last ride, his mom had said.

Suddenly, his stomach aches empty and craves a corndog. He doesn't remember ever letting go of her hand while in line but he must've let go at some point and grabbed the hand of the clown who wasn't really a clown—the man with the bad card trick who gave him the stupid invitation to see something that wasn't even there.

Mom had warned him to stay close and not to wander.

Ian knew the park and could find his way around easily enough, but finding his mom would be like finding his dad's body, which the people looking for him couldn't do after he went over the cliff. Even if he found his mom, she'd be mad and they'd leave early. They wouldn't ride the Ferris wheel as their last ride like she remembered doing with Dad. Ian only had nine tickets anyway since he had dropped one. He holds them to the light, counting again to make sure.

The placid water breaks, enveloping you as you ride the yellow cart beneath the surface. Round you go as the un-reflection of the Ferris wheel above glows through a watery blur. You see them gathered on the pier as the giant the axle turns. A woman and boy embrace—illuminated by a bright disc of moon—and it feels like home.

Though It Rains

The rain won't fall on the both of us
If I pull you in close
And you pull me in close
The sky, although it cries
The sky won't cry on the both of us

And the rain, when it falls
  / Shiver? You won't shiver
  / Take my breath
Such passionate downpours
  / Take my warmth
  / Take my breath
Falling, falling, falling …
  / Quiver? You may quiver

The rain, yes, it will fall
If you're the one I choose
And I'm the one you choose
The sky, yes, it will cry
But it won't cry on the both of us

And the water cascades
  / Tremors! Your heart tremors
  / Take my breath
Redirected showers
  / Take my hand
  / Take my breath
Cascades, cascades, cascades …
  / Hammers! Your heart hammers

The sky won't cry on the both of us
When I pull you in close
And you pull me in close
The rain, although it falls
The rain won't fall on the both of us

I Wanted Black

The crimson balloon pushed through the surface of the puddle with viscous liquid that resembled oil rolling off the glossy rubber. A series of prismatic rings reached out and I heard my father's voice calling for me, silently, as if the balloon was inflating with his last breath and he was trying to say my name but couldn't; like his voice had died years ago, the air from his lungs still trapped inside, pushing the mess of oil on the ground toward me instead.

David, he tried to say.

This wasn't a lucid dream. I thought that too, at first. Lucidity is just a word fabricated for all the people in the world who think the strange things happening around them cannot possibly be real.

David, the balloon tried to say.

It inflated further and spun. A white piece of twine trailed beneath it, pulled taut into the water as if someone below were holding it down.

I reached for the twine and it was like plucking a guitar string. There was definitely something down there, tethering the balloon in place.

Dad, I said. *It's time to let go. You died when I was seven.*

But I knew it was me who needed to let go.

It happened on my birthday. All my friends were there. There were red balloons everywhere: tied onto the backs of the chairs in the dining room, hanging from fan blades, kids running around with them anchored to their wrists, popped ones on the carpet like mottled blood spots. I don't know why my mother chose red. It wasn't my favorite color. My favorite color at the time was black, but she always told me black wasn't a color, it was the absence of color; so I guess she had decided on a real color for me.

I wanted black, Dad, I told the balloon.

The oily substance dripping from the balloon was black and so was the puddle. I touched the balloon and the surface was slick and smelled sweet. Like a kid, I brought my finger to my mouth and tasted it. I don't know why. The flavor reminded me of butter frosting and made me think of the cake.

(Blow out the candles, David)

I counted the candles twice to make sure I was seven. All my friends stood around me in a semicircle, my mother behind me wielding a spatula and knife. She held them skyward with her elbows tucked against her waist. She looked at me like I was her puppy, her head tilted to the side, a wide smile and sparkly teeth.

(Blow them out, David)

My father wasn't home yet. He was supposed to be home by three when the party started. I remember him leaving a few hours earlier and I was mad because he had lied to me. He told me he had to work. He never worked weekends. I knew he was lying because he smiled. There's no way you can look your son in the face and lie to him on his birthday without smiling.

He told me once that the littlest things you do in life impact those around you in ways you may never know, so it is for this reason that everything you do should be backed with love. I was thinking of that when I finally made my wish. I blew out six. The seventh almost went out. It was the sole red one in the mix and it flickered back to life, killing my dreams. I was doing the little things—blowing out a rainbow assortment of cheap candles, wishing for my father to be home. Backed with love.

Wishes only come true if you blow them all out. I remember wax melting onto the butter frosting, red bleeding pink against the white. A part of me hoped that if the flame could flicker back to life, it might flicker back to death. It mocked me. Like the balloons. I wanted to let it burn all the way out, thinking my wish still had a chance if the flame died on its own. And then my mom leaned over my shoulder and blew it out.

That was a long time ago.

The crimson balloon no longer inflated. The oily substance ran the length of the twine to the puddle below. My reflection was concealed somewhere on its surface, the way words hide on paper until you let them out with ink. If I let myself out, the puddle would reveal a seven-year-old boy crying onto his birthday cake.

David, he tried to say.

I didn't want to think about the party, but there it was again.

Someone had knocked on the door and I thought it was him. I knew he had lied about having to go into work and so I thought it might be him returning from the store with a last-minute present. With tears running the course of my red balloon cheeks, I ran to the door.

(Is your mother home?)

A police officer.

(Yes)

My mother, behind me, a hand on my shoulder.

(There's been an accident)

The last thing he ever gave me ...

It's time to let go, David.

He died instantly, the officer told my mother. No pain. I guess it doesn't hurt much to have a car cross the center divider and hit you head-on at freeway speeds. It doesn't hurt to have a steering column pass through your chest. It doesn't hurt to have the lower half of your body severed by an engine block.

It was my birthday and my dad was dead.

David, the balloon tried to say.

I fell to my knees, ran my fingers along the twine. I followed it to the surface of the puddle and let my hand pass through the greasy liquid. It was hot, like blood, and sickly sweet. It coated my hand, my wrist, and then my forearm. I couldn't help but taste it as my lips made contact. My entire arm emerged to find what was holding the balloon in place.

And then I found what I was looking for. Twine was tied around my father's wrist just like the kids at my party.

I don't want them anymore, Dad.

His hand wrapped around mine and squeezed.

Why did you have to lie to me? Why did you go back?

After the accident, police found a portable helium tank and a bag of black balloons in the trunk. He had gone back because I had wanted black. Not red.

The last thing he ever tried to give me was his love.

I don't want them anymore.

The hand beneath the surface let go.

No!

Frantically, I reached for him, his fingers falling away … reaching for me, but falling away. They were too slick and I couldn't hold on. He sank, pulling the twine and the balloon with him. I wrapped my fingers around the twine, but he was too heavy and it slipped through my grasp. The balloon dipped into the oily black puddle and I could finally grab hold of the base.

Stretching tight, it said goodbye with the last of my father's breath.

David, the balloon tried to say.

The twine broke.

The crimson balloon soared to the sun.

Countdown to Null


```
00001111
00001110
00001101
00001100
00001011
00001010
00001001
00001000
00000111
00000110
00000101
00000100
00000011
00000010
00000001
00000000
```

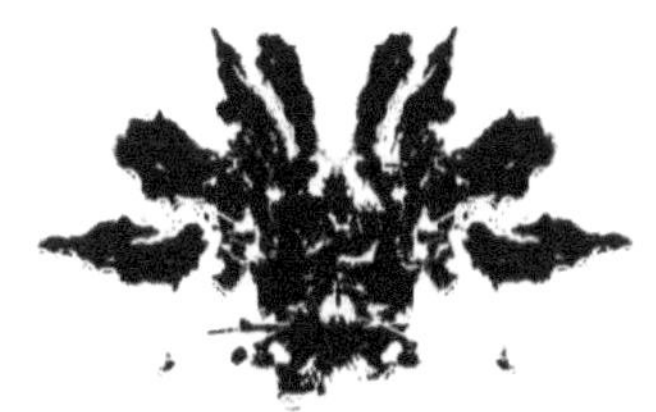

Fireman / Primal Tongue

"Virkeligheden er jo ligesom i eventyrene," said the woman in the terminal.

She smiled and moved her attention to the cooing child in the stroller, then put her hand on the leg of the man sitting next to her, a husband or boyfriend.

Danish. But Gil Sloat couldn't understand a word of it. Were they talking about him?

The man took his turn.

"Jeg håber, du har det dejligt og nyder livet."

Then he chuckled.

"På godt og ondt," she said, taking his hand.

We're in America, people. Speak English.

"NOW BOARDING FLIGHT 0196 TO BALTIMORE / WASHINGTON." A voice layered in static, female; the only airline representative working gate J87. Strange that airports should still use overhead paging to announce flights. Internet and cellular technologies managed ticketing and seating assignments and boarding passes and other travel arrangements, yet a person—an attractive woman in an ugly blue uniform—was still responsible for controlling the chaos of boarding an airplane. Common courtesy and common sense were rarities.

"FREQUENT FLIER PLATINUM MEMBERS MAY BOARD AT THIS TIME."

Most airlines had eliminated First Class, but half a dozen membership programs allowed certain passengers to board before the masses, followed by active duty military, those with disabilities, and families with young children. These minorities then had to luggage-slalom through the impatient herd of coach passengers as they line-hopped to the front.

"THOSE WITH SMARTPHONES, TABLETS AND OTHER HANDHELD DEVICES MAY BOARD AT THIS TIME."

Gil imagined those words over the loudspeaker, followed by the amoeba-like flow of techno-lemmings piling through the gate, smartphones and tablets and other handheld devices aloft to protect them. Shoulders smashing shoulders. Men and women and children trampled by passengers eager to secure their overabundance of carry-on luggage. He imagined standing in back, or seated, like the Danish family, watching the chaos unfold instead of taking part, later to be penalized as his single, size-approved carry-on is checked due to a lack of space in the overhead compartments. He could relate to those people. The patient ones, those he'd *like* to understand. The Danish woman shared his view; he could see it in her eyes.

The rapid boom in technology was partly to blame for the world's ruin. Devices invented to simplify life more often simplified the living. Let a person become dependent on portable technology and then watch him get struck by a vehicle while crossing the street. It happened all the time. The *chinonchest* syndrome: when a person is so involved in their handheld device / gadget / toy, they forget to look up now and again. Zombies, all of them. Keystroke conversations, not spoken word.

And there Gil sat, hearing the words of people he wanted to understand but couldn't. The baby's coos were easier to translate than the Danish. The child wanted attention. Maybe it was foreign cooing.

Is there such a thing? Is all language the same until it's learned? Is there a common language shared by all, perhaps? Something primal, unnecessary to learn, before we fuck it all up and segregate ourselves with language?

"*På godt og ondt,*" Gil said, copying what the woman had said.

She looked up from the child.

He hadn't meant to speak the unfamiliar phrase, but the terminal was so dead with people not talking that the words came out of his mouth, as if wanting to be heard.

"*Taler du dansk?*"

A question. Somehow he knew she asked if he understood Danish; that much he could gather by facial movements and her curiosity.

Her husband nodded. "*God eftermiddag!*"

"Sorry," Gil said, embarrassed. "I don't speak Danish."

The woman's eyebrows furrowed. She spoke slowly: "But you know what was I said, in *dansk*. 'For better or worse,' you said."

Why do so few Americans learn other languages?

Her English wasn't perfect, but she had translated his words and could speak the language far better than his butchery of *dansk*, of which he understood zilch.

Gil apologized again. "I repeated the words because I enjoyed the sound. I only know English. What was that first thing you said? *Virkeli*-something …"

"*Virkeligheden er jo ligesom i eventyrene.*" The words rolled easily off her tongue, with elegance and grace.

"Sounds beautiful. What does it mean?"

"Haha. It means—" Her eyes searched the ceiling, "I guess you could say: what is real is like the fairy tales."

"If only that were—"

"PASSENGERS WITH SPECIAL NEEDS AND THOSE WITH CHILDREN CAN NOW BOARD."

The passengers without special needs, and the childless, sandwiched closer to the front.

Gil had special needs. He needed to understand.

Maybe people don't want to understand.

The Danish couple rose, searching for a path.

The husband shrugged his shoulders. "Eh," he said. "Plane will not leave without."

Seeing the couple made him feel alone. If only he and Nell were still together, he could stand by her side, hold her hand. Gil wore happiness like a mask and Nell ran off with it. He could no longer hide depression from the world …

"MICHAEL RILEY, PLEASE REPORT TO THE PODIUM. MICHAEL RILEY, PLEASE REPORT TO THE PODIUM FOR YOUR STANDBY SEATING ASSIGNMENT."

"Well," Gil said. "It looks like this is going to take some—"

"ACTIVE DUTY MILITARY MAY BOARD AT THIS TIME, FOLLOWED BY …" The gate agent clicked off, covered the handset to help a customer—apparently not Michael Riley, unless he was a heavyset black woman with a cane—before starting again.

"BY ZONE 1. ZONE 1 MAY BOARD AT THIS TIME."

So many detailed instructions, yet no one listened.

"This is going to take a while," Gil said. "I'm going to find some coffee and learn another language."

"*Ét sprog er aldrig nok,*" the woman said.

Language translation apps were inexpensive if you already owned a mobile device, but they rarely made the bestseller list. Such spots were apparently reserved for entertainment and educational packages. Those apps should raise the bar; instead, they seemed to make everyone *stupider*, as Nell used to say.

Gil bought a paltry vanilla latte—the last time he'd ever settle for coffee from one of the Starbucks machines—as he browsed the programs available at the *A.I. Unlimited* kiosk: an unmanned touchscreen mounted on a wall three gates down from J87. A scanner read payments, and a retractable cable connected to one's *Digital Software Adaptation Interface.* *D-SAI* for short.

At the top of the list was a flashbook of *Fahrenheit 451*, which was amusing: the Ray Bradbury classic about a world where books were burned out of existence, only to be preserved by those willing to memorize them. The eBook version issued twenty years ago had made Gil laugh—paper pages turned / burned to digital—but that was during the push to eliminate paper. People still read then.

Once the eBook craze dwindled—following criminalization of printing on paper—and people could simply upload stories into their minds without needing to read them, the concept of 'reading' died. For most people, anyway. Gil still 'read' and enjoyed it, although the stories *he* read were digital. He saw it as a vacation from reality; to be lost in the pages of fiction, immersed in characterization and plot. *That* was a liberating experience.

The line at J87 was a mess. Twenty minutes to board.

He'd never tried a flashbook. What was the point?

It had been years since he'd read Bradbury. He remembered the highlights, such as 'firemen' raiding houses to confiscate books and set them on fire, and classic books memorized word for word by a rebellious few. Most memories of the book seemed to have burned as well.

Why not buy a copy?

The screen scrolled through simple instructions.

Gil attached the *D-SAI* cable to the port on his left wrist, twisting until it locked in place.

Ray would be rolling over in his grave if he saw this …

Perhaps he had envisioned it.

Gil pressed the button and waited.

UPLOADING … TRANSACTION COMPLETE.

Instantaneously, Gil remembered the missing pieces, the novel suddenly whole. In only a moment, the words were there.

"It was a pleasure to burn," he recited to no one. "It was a special pleasure to see things eaten, to see things blackened and changed. With the brass nozzle in his fists, with this great python spitting its venomous kerosene upon the world, the blood pounded in his hands, and his hands were the hands of some amazing conductor playing all the symphonies of blazing and burning to bring down the tatters and charcoal ruins of history."

The entire book.

Gil, the technology proselyte.

For the next month, the book would be his, word for word. That's how the copyright-protected apps worked. The words still belonged to Bradbury's estate. Someone, somewhere, would receive a paltry stipend for this purchase. After the virtual rental, whatever Gil had read and could remember would remain. But the experience was shortened from hours to milliseconds, which defeated the purpose of reading—the long escape from reality reduced to a hiccup.

Such an amazing book.

Educational material was much different. The purchaser became the owner—there was no expiration—and permanent knowledge was retained. The books were uploaded to one's long-term memory as opposed to short-term memory, a different part of the brain.

This meant more money.

Digital education courses were priced higher than classes taken in person. Language *translation* programs worked on a temporary basis for travel or whatnot, with the purchaser comprehending the spoken word of another language but unable to speak it. Language *knowledge* programs worked on a permanent basis, with the purchaser understanding the new language indefinitely. It was expensive, however. Basic Spanish, the second most common language in the United States, cost more than learning four years of Spanish in college, and that was only for comprehension. Languages still required linguistic practice—learned muscle memory of the tongue and mouth—as well as phonological and morphological development to speak, read, and write. But you couldn't upload those, and no one wrote anymore.

Gil's savings could buy him only a single permanent language; that, and his trip to Europe. He was running from life, but it was a much-needed vacation. It would help him forget.

For three weeks, he'd travel to Portugal, Spain, France, and then through Belgium, Amsterdam, and Germany, perhaps with a stop at Denmark before crossing over to Sweden. The Baltimore / Washington International Airport was his first destination, then a thirteen hour nonstop flight to Lisbon.

Gil touched the display and purchased 30-day rentals of Spanish / *español*, French / *le français*, German / *Deutsch*, Swedish / *svenska*, Danish / *dansk*, and Portuguese / *português*.

After Portuguese, the screen flickered with a glitch of ones and zeros and returned to a confirmation screen. After hesitating, he pressed the button labeled UPLOAD ALL.

"Hmm." He felt nothing.

As a test, Gil changed the language settings on the kiosk to Spanish / *español*. The words all changed. The center of the display read:

¿HABLA USTED ESPAÑOL? SÍ / NO

"Technically, I do not *speak* Spanish, but why not?" He recognized the phrase from his newly-purchased memory. He pressed the button and said, "Sí."

SELECCIONE EN EL MENÚ SIGUIENTE, POR FAVOR

"Please select from the menu below. Incredible ..." He tried repeating the phrase, but butchered the hell out of it, getting only *por favor* correct, since he'd heard that before, like the French *s'il vous plait*.

"*Sa-lid-a*," he said, pressing the Exit button.

The chaotic line at gate J87 had become manageable, so he headed in that direction and joined the line. There were maybe twenty people left to board. The gate agent hassled the Danish couple about the stroller, for not boarding earlier when she'd called for families with young children. Gil didn't need a translator program to decipher the gestures from the woman in the ugly blue uniform.

A commotion at the *A.I. Unlimited* kiosk turned him around. A squad of uniformed men with assault rifles surrounded the device while two men in suits inspected the screen. Others in suits wandered the terminal, interviewing those in the area, fingers to their ears. One made eye contact with Gil before he boarded.

"*Humea samaj mei nai aweh. Kai koy nai beil khoweh?*"

That's how it sounded, at least.

Gil recognized the dialect as Indian vernacular: Hindi, Marathi, Bengali, or Punjabi. Probably Hindi.

The rapid speech pattern made him think of Nell, a strikingly beautiful woman he'd met in Quebec. Although Nell spoke fluent English, her second language, she had to keep reminding Gil to speak more slowly. *Translation takes time*, she had said. He didn't realize how quick-spoken English sounded to the world outside his bubble until he met her. Not until she rattled off *le français* to prove a point: "*Comment vas-tu? Je vais bien, merci. Et toi? Comme-ci, comme-ça. Quoi de neuf?* You understood only a few of those words. It seemed normal to me, but to you it seemed fast, *correct?*"

Nell's last words to him: "Are you happy?"

Of course I'm happy, he'd said, taking her words out of context, not realizing she was saying goodbye. *Does she think I'm not?*

They were lines from Bradbury.

It was a pleasure to burn, it was a pleasure to—

01110011 01100101 01100101 00100000
01110100 01101000 01101001 01101110
01100111 01110011 00100000 01100101
01100001 01110100 01100101 01101110

—to see things blackened and changed.

Perhaps an error in the flashbook.

The Indian fellows next to him rambled untranslatable phrases. Even if he could understand, the words would probably get lost in translation.

"Hamar kayneh kali yeh hai: Hindustani longh Gita mei yeh baath par ke samjis ke beil nai khowa jai. Maine para aur samjah ke har zindagi ek tofah hai. Kitna kitabh, jaise Quran aur Bible mei sawal likhan hai, aur insan par ke soche ke yei such baath hai? Tabh ye baath insan apan aur apan bachei ke zindagi mei likh ..."

The older one looked at Gil.

"My little brother, he thinks I want to eat our mother. Ha! Mothers give you milk, and so do cows; that's his reasoning. Since I like quarter-pounders with cheese," he said, lifting the bag, "he thinks I'd butcher our mother."

"That's not what I said."

"He thinks the Gita says we shouldn't eat beef, even though it was written before we ever had McDonald's."

"Don't listen to him. *Gita kuch aur nai bole iske bareh mei.* He's putting words in my mouth."

"He puts goat in his mouth. Hindustani people eat goats, and goats give milk. He has no justification for his reasoning. Do you eat goat?"

Gil shrugged. "Can't say I've ever had the opportunity."

"Tastes like old beef." The older brother removed the hamburger from the bag. He unwrapped half of it and took a big, slow bite. After washing it down with soda, he said, "Cow is much tastier than goat, whether or not the Gita says so."

"FLIGHT ATTENDANTS, PREPARE FOR TAKE-OFF."

The plane lurched as it was pushed back from the gate.

Gil had read that planes did not have a means of moving in reverse. They had to be pushed by something more primitive—a ground-based vehicle, something capable of bidirectional movement, translating *reverse*, one could say.

After take-off, the brothers conversed again in Hindi.

Should have picked up that language too, instead of this faulty book.

Gil loved theoretical / religious arguments, something everyone struggled with. The struggle intrigued him.

He asked the older brother, "Do they still teach writing where you're from?"

"I am from California, so no."

"Ah, sorry."

Following in the wake of other nations, public schools in the United States had stopped teaching writing over two decades ago; instead, language education focused on typing, whether by keyboard or touchscreen. The world had migrated to a digital age. Unless purchased from art supply stores, pencils and pens were a rarity, and writing on paper was unheard of. Cursive had been the first to go—schools stopped teaching it. The act of writing was a lost skill.

"But if you mean India, the answer is also no."

"It's a shame, really."

"Yes, it is … but, like with *all* change, we can choose not to accept it. Do you write?"

"I write every day," Gil said, "at least a page. My mother encouraged writing. And she saw it coming. 'Soon,' she told me, 'the world will no longer have a need for books or writing of any kind.' For her *last* birthday, I bought her one of those Kindle devices, one of the first eBooks. She unwrapped it, held it like fragile glass and said, 'What in God's name is this?' She used it once, I think, but said she'd rather stick to 'real' books. That she liked the feel of them, the smell of their pages."

"What did she do when they stopped printing books?"

"She said no one writes worth a damn anymore, and that *real* writers had created enough books for generations to read. 'We don't need new books,' she said. 'Everything that *can* be written *has* been written. Everything new plagiarizes from the past. Nothing new is original.'"

"What is it you write?"

"My own take on unoriginal ideas. She gave me these journals years ago. Black leather-bound with two hundred pages in each. I'm not sure where she found them, but she gave me about twenty. I've filled up five so far. Who knows, maybe someday I'll do something with them."

"Do you have a pen?"

Gil carried one in his pocket—nearly confiscated at

security. He pulled it free, clicked the end, handed it to him.

"My brother," he said, pointing with his thumb, "he cannot write. He can copy what he sees, like drawing shapes, but he cannot really write. Our mother taught me and my sisters, though. My grammar is horrible, I must warn you."

On the back of his drink napkin, in smooth script, he wrote some words in hindi:

भाषा के बिना मनुष्य कभी नहीं छोड़ा जाएगा

"It's beautiful. What does it mean?"
"Man will never be left without language."

Halfway through a ginger ale and an unfunny romantic comedy on the seat monitors—soundless because he wasn't interested—the Starbucks coffee wanted out. Whenever Gil needed to use the restroom on flights, he was never alone. A line of three needed to un-Starbucks their bladders.

He excused himself as he squeezed by the Indian brothers and joined the end of the line. As he moved up the aisle, he hoped to hear one of the languages he had purchased so he could understand the translation process. Most passengers were engrossed in the movie, occupied with handheld devices or otherwise silent.

That's what the world's becoming. Silent.

After a dance with an overweight fellow returning to his seat, Gil noticed the Danish couple at the back of the plane.

As Gil moved closer, he was able to understand their conversation, as if by telepathy or by mental teleprompter:

"Jeg begik en fejl," the woman said. I made a mistake.

"Det kan man vist roligt sige." I'll say.

"Hvad mener du?" What do you mean?

"Det, jeg siger." What I am saying.

"Men du er jo nødt til at tilgive mig, hvis vi skal komme videre." But you have to forgive me, if we are to move on.

Forgive her for what? What could she have possibly done?

She touched her husband's hand, but he pulled away and turned to the window. She looked at Gil, but didn't smile this time. He felt pity, then guilt for listening in to this private conversation.

They were going through what he'd gone through months before with Nell. Their body language told him they'd fallen apart.

They were at the end of something once wonderful.

"Det ved jeg ikke, om jeg kan," the Danish man said. I don't know if I can do that.

"Jamen, hvad vil du så?" Well, what do you want then?

"Lige nu vil jeg bare have, at du ikke siger noget." Right now, I want you to not say anything.

The Danish couple's fairytale relationship was just that: a fairytale. Whether or not Gil wanted to listen, he was going hear and understand their conversation. From their meeting at the gate, they believed he couldn't comprehend their language, and probably assumed others couldn't, either.

Gil felt wrong, but he couldn't turn it off. He focused his attention elsewhere, feigning ignorance, looking to the signs that read NO SMOKING and NO E-SMOKING, to the personal air vents and flight attendant call buttons and the overhead compartments, anything to hold his attention other than their words. He wanted to return to his seat, to hold his bladder longer, but the line had filled in behind him and he was trapped.

If he could turn back time, he'd return the language.

"Hold nu op. Alle begår fejl. Vi er kun mennesker. Og hvis vi ikke kan tilgive, hvor ender vi så?" Come on. Everybody makes mistakes. We are only human. And if we can't forgive, then where do we end?

Perhaps she'd cheated on him. But it was none of Gil's business.

He massaged his temples, trying not to listen, trying not to remember Nell, trying instead to recall the back of the Sky Mall digizine from the pouch in his seat—an advertisement for a perfume with a horizontal half-naked couple on a beach with a caption proclaiming the name of the perfume and a tide frozen in time, indefinitely lapping at their bodies. A fake-perfect, half-naked couple colliding on the sand in halftones with an illuminated heart-shaped bottle in the foreground, yet the words—

"Ti nu stille," he said. Be quiet.

Words ever so right.

Gil tried to bring up the book, to hide in the digital pages stored in his mind, but the words weren't there.

Bradbury was gone.

"Så det er det?" So that's it then?

"Måske." Maybe.

"Skal jeg gå?" Do you want me to leave?

He'd said the same thing to Nell. Different words, but the same words.

"Nogle gange er fejl så store, at de ikke kan tilgives. Vil du ikke nok tie stille. Jeg har brug for at tænke." Sometimes mistakes are so big, that they cannot be forgiven. Please be quiet. I need

to think.

"Undskyld. Jeg mener det virkelig. Hvis jeg kunne gøre det om, ville jeg gøre det. Undskyld." I'm sorry. I really mean it. If I could do it over, I would. I'm sorry.

"Tak." Thanks.

Gil shuffled forward.

The Danish woman caught him trying not to look at her this time and smiled, but the passion hidden in that smile did not need translation: *passion* meant *suffering*. He saw it in her eyes. They were only dry because hurt welled in place of tears. She turned to her husband, who gave his attention to the white blanket of cloud outside the window. So she focused on the child between them. That's when the corners of her mouth curled and she silently cried, a single tear dripping onto her lap.

The primal language.

Action and *reaction. Feeling. Emotion.*

The baby cooing and the mother's instinctual response of tending to a child too young for dialogue, just *goo-goos* and *ga-gas* and other nonsensical noises. Pets cuddling when you're sick, acting sad when you're sad, happy when you're happy. A baby crying because another baby is crying. Sadness answering sadness, anger countering anger, joy begetting joy, a smile met with another smile …

Tongues only wrought confusion.

Virkeligheden er jo ligesom i eventyrene, she'd said to Gil at the gate. He understood now. People often lived the fairy tale life, masking misery with ideals of happiness. Words that once sounded beautiful now sounded terrible. They sounded familiar.

He offered the woman a crooked smile, hoping she'd

look up from her sorrow to see that *he* understood; to see empathy—something they could communicate without the need for words.

I don't want them anymore.

After touching down in Portugal, he couldn't sleep. His mind would not shut off. Every conversation required his attention, no matter the language, whether he wanted to hear or not.

All at once the pages of the flashbook returned.

To quiet the endless conversations translating through his mind, mixtures of Spanish-Portuguese-English-French, Gil referenced *Fahrenheit 451*, recalling and reciting the words as if one of its memorizing characters.

"The woman's hand twitched on the single matchstick," he said. "The fumes of kerosene bloomed up about her … felt the hidden book pound like a heart against his—"

01100011 01101000 01100101 01110011
01110100 00001101 00001010

What's wrong with this damn thing?

A woman wanted his attention, to ask him something, directions perhaps.

He kept walking out of the Lisbon terminal.

"Silly words, silly words, silly awful hurting words …"

Gil skipped ahead to a favorite part: the end.

"And when it came to his turn, what could he say, what could he offer on a day like this, to make the trip a little easier? To everything there is a season. Yes. A time to break down, and a time to build up. Yes. A time to keep silence, and a time to speak. Yes, all that. But what else. What else? Something, something …"

A man standing next to a white Mercedes with a lit TÁXI roof ornament hailed him down the moment he stepped out of the Lisbon terminal.

"*Americano, americano! Senhor, you need taxi?*"

Do I look that American?

"*Que hotel?*"

"Which hotel?" He checked his cellphone. "Yes, it's uh … here it is. Sofitel Lisbon Liberdade."

"Sofitel Lisbon, nice … *cinco estrelas.*" The driver held out his hands. "*Dar!*" Give!

Give?

The man shook his hands for the luggage, and Gil understood without needing the words, which didn't do him much good when translated; he was having trouble keeping up. *Cinco estralas,* the man said, meaning the hotel: *five stars.*

"Yes. Thank you," Gil said, handing over his suitcases.

Translation takes time, Nell's voice haunted.

"*Obrigado.*" Thank you.

"*Obrigado.*"

The cabbie opened the trunk, tossed his luggage inside. Gil made his way into the backseat, where he was surprised to find a man already seated.

"*Ei.*" Hey.

Gil nodded. The man nodded. The doors closed, and that was that. Then something hot speared his leg in a way that made his muscles spasm and his jaw clamp.

"*Ser ainda,*" the man said. Be still.

He had buried the needle of a large syringe deep into

Gil's thigh as the taxi sped away. The barrel stuck from his leg like a knife hilt. Gil controlled his eyes, but the rest of his body was paralyzed; not numb, because the liquid burned along his leg, up into his groin, and blossomed in his chest. The sensation crawled up his neck. He'd clenched his teeth at the initial agony and now his mouth was stuck shut, lips tight. Gil tried to scream at the reflection of the taxi driver, but the taxi driver smiled and repositioned the mirror so that Gil stared at himself.

They were going to jack him, and there was nothing he could do about it.

The man next to him felt Gil's pocket and pulled out his handheld. He positioned it in front of Gil's face to unlock it with facial recognition security. Within seconds, he brought up Gil's digital passport and banking information and scanned them into an antiquated touchscreen device.

"We're sorry to do this to you, Americano. You have made recent purchases, no? *Tradução para a língua.*" Language translation.

Gil's sealed mouth made untranslatable noises.

"Our *amigo entende* Portuguese."

"*Vamos,* Abrahan," said the driver. Let's go.

Abrahan didn't translate to anything. It was his name.

"Bad luck for you, *meu amigo,*" said the man next to him. He pressed the handheld to Gil's face, close enough to make it blurry and unreadable.

"*Lamentamos muito, meu amigo,*" the driver said. We are very sorry, my friend.

"You found something you weren't supposed to find. *Dados sensíveis.*" Sensitive data. "But your find is, how do you say ... *inestimável?*" Invaluable.

Hidden code in the book?

"Now in here," Abrahan said, tapping Gil's forehead. "We can leave no trace."

The phone display turned white and then it was gone, black, powerless, and Gil knew it had been wiped clean.

"Fazer a conexão," the driver said. Make the connection.

"Yeah, yeah," Abrahan said.

"Apagá-lo." Erase him.

The most frightening phrase Gil had ever heard.

Two words.

No, no, no—

Abrahan prepared a *black box*—an unethical device used by computer hackers long ago, the plain chassis hiding the complex interior, an interface on either side.

He attached a cable to the *D-SAI* port on Gil's wrist and connected the other end to the black box. The antiquated touchscreen connected to the interface to decode the digital makeup of whatever he planned to wipe from Gil's mind.

How much could he see? What could he erase?

And then the man told him.

"Language translation app: *português*, language translation app: *español*, language translation app: *le français, Deutsch, svenska, dansk* … You must like languages, *meu amigo*. Ah, flashbook: *Fahrenheit 451. Bom livro?"* Good book?

The fireman.

"Find it?" said the driver.

"Sim." Yeah.

The man worked through the list of languages, swiping his finger across each program to erase them: *"Dansk, ido."* Gone. *"Svenska, ido. Deutsch, ido. Le français, ido. Español, ido."* His finger simply flicked them away. *"Português,"* he said and paused. "I take this one, you no longer *entender* ..."

"Não se preocupe." Don't worry. "I will let you keep *bom livro* to have until you pass, but will scramble the rest. *Entender* scramble, *como ovos?"* Like eggs.

They planned to erase Gil's memory; not just the translation applications or past purchases, but everything.

"Wrong place, wrong time, *meu amigo.* We have to destroy it all. You will not feel a thing, *eu prometo."* I promise. *"Português, ido,"* he said, swiping his finger one last time, and it was gone. All his learned languages were gone.

A small part of Gil welcomed the loss.

"Fazê-lo," the driver said. No translation.

"Não me apresse. Isto é difícil."

"Você já fez isso antes."

"Cem vezes."

Foreign words once again.

The driver pulled the car into an empty alley. They gently carried Gil's numb body and set him on the pavement. Immobile, he faced the sun as they poured flammables over his body and his belongings.

Kerosene is nothing but perfume to me ... part of the book.

Abrahan tapped on the device still connected to the port on Gil's wrist, deleting, erasing, doing something ...

"Lamentamos muito, meu amigo."

Soon it would—

01001001 00100000 01101100 01101111
01110110 01100101 00100000 01111001
01101111 01110101 00101100 00100000
01001110 01100101 01101100 01101100
00101110

—be gone, perhaps a virus shot through the mind to—
"Sinto muito," one of them said.
Nell—

01001001 01100110 00100000 01110011
01101111 01101101 01100101 01101111
01101110 01100101 00100000 01110011
01101111 01101101 01100101 01101000
01101111 01110111 00100000 01100110
01101001 01101110 01100100 01110011
00100000 01110100 01101000 01101001
01110011 00100000 01101100 01101111
01110011 01110100 00100000 01110100
01101000 01101111 01110101 01100111
01101000 01110100 00100000 01100001
01101101 01101001 01100100 00100000
01100001 00100000 01100010 01101001
01101110 01100001 01110010 01111001
00100000 01110111 01101111 01110010
01101100 01100100 00101100 00100000
01101011 01101110 01101111 01110111
00100000 01110100 01101000 01100001
01110100 00100000 01001001 00100000
01101000 01100001 01110110 01100101
00100000 01100001 01101100 01110111
01100001 01111001 01110011 00100000
01101100 01101111 01110110 01100101
01100100 00100000 01111001 01101111
01110101 00101110

PART ONE

The Hearth and the Salamander

It was a pleasure to burn.

It was a special pleasure to see things eaten, to see things blackened and *changed*. With the brass nozzle in his fists, with this great python spitting its venomous kerosene upon the world, the blood pounded in his hands, and his hands were the hands of some amazing conductor playing all the symphonies of blazing and burning to bring down the tatters and charcoal ruins of history …

Not Responding

243

Retry copy? (y/n)

Dandelion Clocks

"Unfortunately, the clock is ticking, the hours are
going by. The past increases, the future recedes.
Possibilities decreasing, regrets mounting."
– Haruki Murakami, *Dance Dance Dance*

"Time is what stops history happening at once;
time is the speed at which the past disappears."
– David Mitchell, *Cloud Atlas*

"Everything in life is just for a while."
– Philip K. Dick, *A Scanner Darkly*

1990 (17)

Ash materialized from the cloud-hidden tops of sky-scrap-
ers and fluttered down, or perhaps up, to the gray blanket
covering a ground that had become her sky. The buildings
protruded from the white earth like massive, multi-win-
dowed stalactites, or stalagmites, depending on perspective:
elongated, three-dimensional checkerboards of glass and

concrete, one after the other after the other, from every direction.

Lanie swung by her knees from the lowest pull-up bar, the wet tip of her ponytail dangling to brushstroke the flowers beneath her. She had flipped upside-down to paint the world in a different image. Next to the swings was a fairy fountain that no longer worked. As far as she could remember, in her seventeen years, it had never worked.

She dropped a single drop of *D5* into each eye and welcomed the rush.

1993 (20)

The City's 'new teeth,' her ex-roomie Nicole had called the buildings. Nic never called The City by its name, even though they'd moved into the apartment a week ago. "They're always growing in somewhere, places they shouldn't, mayhap, layers of 'em, the old ones making way for the new. Old ones crumbling down so newer, taller, shinier ones can go up. This city's got bite," she'd said. She knew everything there was to know about The City because she had books on the coffee table better suited for hotel lobbies.

Although Nic was from Seattle, and sometimes over-pronounced words like 'wash' to 'warsh' and under-pronounced words like 'school' to 'schoo,' she often absorbed accents of those around her. Before she'd gone on the 'new teeth' spiel, she'd been talking with some guy on the phone she referred to as Bee, or B, the letter, and he'd spoken loudly enough through the phone so that Lanie could tell he was a southerner. He had some sort of undisclosed relationship with Nic, and used words like 'mayhap.'

Could have been the drugs or the sex that made him call. Could have been B knowing something more about Lanie, about Hopkins House, where she was still admitted so she could "reintegrate with society," as one of the caregivers had so eloquently put it, or that people were looking for her because she'd been gone for three weeks. Or he could have told her about the scars. "You cut yourself or something?" Nic had asked when they'd first met.

2003 (30)

The same pull-up bar, thirteen years later. Still there after all these years, only aged, thirteen years. *Wonder how many have used it?* She could ask of herself the same thing.

Pull up if I pull up, she mused.

Alone in the park, no one watched her grab hold of the bar, hoist her feet up and bend her knees around the metal. Thirty years old and still monkeying around. Her hands let go and her body swayed. *Upside-down and all around*, she thought. Out of habit, she reached for her pocket, expecting the Visine bottle laced with *D5*. The world had looked so beautiful, then, through psychedelic haze.

Gray, rotted teeth, Lanie thought, staring down at the buildings through dry eyes.

She thought of frowning, but knew it would look like a smile to those right-side-up, and no one in The City smiled much anymore.

The towers once stood in view of where she dangled. Now the lot was a hole in the ground where people were trying to rebuild something bigger so The City could bite harder.

She imagined those final jumpers before the great collapse—collaps*es*—and the bodies falling up instead, leaping back into the building, the smoke un-billowing, the fires un-burning, the planes un-crashing into them, the day returning to the peaceful norm that existed up until that exact moment. Less than two years ago.

She imagined Nicole—one of the small blackbirds flying in the sky that morning—body cartwheeling in reverse, un-falling. If she rewound the memories, Lanie could rewrite their final conversation, of which she remembered every word, and

> *fuck you* could be changed,
> *get out* could be changed,
> *no!* could be changed, and all the hate behind it,
> *don't wanna see you when I get back* could be changed,
> *not friends* could be changed,
> *not—*

1990 (17)

Ash continued to fall / rise.

Tears un-welled.

Lanie's fingers had pruned in the cold, and, perhaps with too much blood flowing to her head from hanging upside-down for so long, a whitish aura wafted from her hands, as if moving them caused the air around her fingers to breathe. Maybe it was the drugs. She let out her own breath, a funnel of warm air, which disappeared up / down into the sky / ground like the skyscrapers. Buildings bit into the ground, burying the people inside.

2003 (30)

The world right-sided as Lanie reached for the pull-up bar and slid her legs free. She was done dangling. She could no longer paint her mirror-flipped world, not without help. The sky became ground and the ground the sky, both whitish-gray and blinding and smelling of ozone. She grabbed a frozen dandelion at her feet and brought the broken stem to her nose to replace the smell with something poignant. Snow fluttered around her, not ash, although it *had* ashed once.

2001 (28)

She had walked the kid she was mentoring from school because the schools had let out before they began; the poor sap's mom was drunk and Lanie was his sometimes babysitter when she was out of Hopkins House long enough to make some money. Lanie and dozens of the kid's classmates walked together down Church Street, toting backpacks, ten or so blocks from the real reason why they were sent home early. Some of the younger kids were confused because it wasn't snowing enough for a snow day; it wasn't even cold, but full sun, not a cloud in the sky, although it was overcast and white fell around them.

Lanie remembered holding out her hand to catch a flake and one landed on the tip of her middle finger. She was tempted to make a wish and blow at it, like a dandelion clock, her nickname for the white puffs left behind by the dead yellow flowers—rumored to give the time of day based on the number of puffs it took to blow all the wisps away; instead, she had rubbed the flake with her thumb and watched it turn gray, and smelled campfire.

Then it had really started to come down, covering the children, ash falling around them like someone in Lower Manhattan had blown the world's largest dandelion clocks from the tallest towers in The City. Soon, they were breathing ash, tasting it, leaving behind footprints as the sirens wailed. One child, too young to understand, had lain down to make an ash angel. Some of the innocent children laughed and threw clumps.

What Lanie hadn't known, then, what none of them understood until later, was the stuff in which they played, the stuff they had tasted and had worn, what had coated their skin and bittered their tongues, was composed of something not-so-fun, perhaps the dead, even. Perhaps her friend Nic.

The only good to come from that day was that race had disappeared, if only for a moment, leaving behind a single, united people wearing identical ash skin.

Lanie traded the dandelion for one of the clocks, brought it to her lips, and blew. Three in the afternoon, the flower told her. White puffs swirled around, taken by the wind.

1980 (7)

"What time is it?" said a man with a faceless face—
    [a breath / a puff]
        and voiceless voice—
    At least one o'clock.
    "What time is it?"

[a breath / a puff]
>> too soft to recognize.
At least two o'clock.
"What time is it?"
>> [a breath / a puff]
>> The same words: familiar, yet unfamiliar.
At least three o'clock.

2003 (30)

Memories wouldn't flow back that far. Perhaps they stayed behind on the asphalt following the accident because she remembered only the dandelion clocks. The watch on her wrist ticked three o'clock. Snow collected on the frozen ground as she searched for the missing parts of her childhood.

1979 (6)

Nothing there.

1978 (5)

Nothing there.

1977 (4)

Nothing there.
>> Nothing there.
>> Nothing there.
>> Nothing there.

2003 (30)

Four years old was as far back as Lanie tried to remember, but there was nothing there, either, so she moved ahead, to just before the accident, to the fragments: a man's face, as common as any other, featureless, unremarkable; his name, Black, like the memory (or was that the uniformed man?); one red, untied Converse on the sidewalk, marking the site of impact; the swerve of tire tread trailing from street curb to lawn to fence and back to the street again.

1988 (15)

This was before Nic, before experimenting with *D5*, and before Hopkins House had taken her as prisoner, or 'permanent resident' as some of the girls called it. Transformers and Star Wars and Matchbox were popular among boys, and My Little Pony and Cabbage Patch dolls attracted the girls; Pepsi and Budweiser cans were mostly white and cigarettes were allowed in public; most importantly, this was a time when 'older' cars were made more of metal than plastics or fiberglass, before things like crash star ratings and 'crumple zones' and airbags and laminated safety glass.

The silver Buick hit Lanie with enough force to send her over the front bumper and headfirst through the windshield, crumpling / bending her in half as her legs caught in the passenger seat headrest, her left hand swinging wildly to bury itself in the driver's face. Most of Lanie landed in the backseat. Her Schwinn with rainbow ribbons on the handlebars went beneath the bumper, dragging for half a block, eventually smashing flat until escaping the undercarriage.

Lanie would have died if the car was newer, and the driver would have survived, instead of the other way around.

In a better-painted world, the driver would have walked away, protected by a spider web of glass and a crumpled front bumper and hood, with Lanie smashed against the windshield, or perhaps redirected by impact. But the car was old and like God and unforgiving, and the driver died, left behind in this world with a crater for a face while his Buick only needed Bondo, sanding and touch-up paint. In a newer, better-painted world, Lanie would have died.

The last sounds she heard from her childhood, which at that chaotic moment transformed into the first sounds she would ever clearly remember hearing in life: metal on cement as the heavy Buick scraped the curb, and the crack of a windshield. Her last / first visuals, both via the rear window: her red Converse shoes—one on the sidewalk half a block back, the other a dim reflection, somehow behind her and caught in the headrest.

A man sat next to her in the backseat and he unbuckled. Lanie tried to remember an empty, not-there face, a smooth flap of white surrounded by a muddy gray aura. Blood from the driver's face, from Lanie's fist smashing into it, speckled the flat skin where his face should have been. If the man next to her could have shown emotion, it would have disclosed fear: not from the accident, nor from Lanie crumpled up next to him on the bench seat like a rag doll, but over the driver's condition, which, if the faceless man had had eyes, he would have seen reflected from the rear view mirror. Perhaps the muddy gray was the fear smoking out of him. He smeared red and matter with the back of his wrist.

Lanie's trembling hand reached for him, but he pushed her bloody hand aside. When he spoke, the intense drone in her ears absorbed his mouthless words—a violinist holding a high-pitched note. He pulled a pocketknife and unfolded the blade. He pushed the metal into Lanie's neck to the hilt and twisted, slid it free, and then did the same to her chest until air escaped her lungs.

Collapsing, she had thought.

She reached for him again, but he didn't want to touch her with anything other than metal. He cut her wrist with crisscrosses deep enough to well and spurt red over him anyway. The aura surrounding him darkened to almost black, and it thickened. His face slightly reformed from the blank canvas to reveal he was scared and then it was gone again. He slashed one last time at her face before turning away from her and letting himself out of the Buick with the fear smoke trailing after him.

Lanie's world whitened.

Everything before the accident was muddled. Everything after was life and all that mattered. Did everything before the accident matter? Perhaps some of it mattered, but, like The City, it was covered in ash.

2001 (28)

Collapsing, she thought.

In the distance, behind the haze, small blackbirds fell from the sky.

Cartwheeling, she thought.

Red dragons with white ladder spines roared by on the street, one after the other, close enough to the sidewalk to pull the air and suck a few of the children nearly into the gutters with their hot breath. One child, a kindergarten boy, lost his camouflage backpack, which tumbled beneath the black-blur feet of the third beast.

"Nicole," she said to one of the children, a girl of seven with strawberry blonde hair pulled back in a braid, and with asymmetric freckles, three on one cheek, two on the other. "I mean your mom, which one does she—?"

And then the second building—

1983 (10)

Some familiar yet unfamiliar building burning to the ground, crackling, popping, a glowing orange skeleton of framework, smoke, the numbers 196 dangling above the door, swinging, falling to—

"What time is it?"

[a breath / a puff]

the ground next to a toy airplane (no, a black SR-71 jet) someone stepped on as they ran from the flames, Lanie's hair singed and charred nearly to the scalp, a child screaming, *children* screaming, adults herding, auras billowing from bodies, windows exploding, sirens wailing, a book of matches in the pocket of her jeans, pressing against—

At least four o'clock.

"What time is it?"

[a breath / a puff]

her leg, sulfuric fingertips, an unrecognizable woman completely on fire, rolling onto the grass, catching everything around her on fire and—

At least five o'clock.

"What time is it?"
    [a breath / a puff]
        screaming. So much screaming.
  At least six o'clock.

1988 (15)

A blurry clock on the wall in her hospital room ticked six o'clock and she somehow knew it was the morning six o'clock, not the dinnertime six o'clock.

Equal-sized blurry bags of raspberry syrup and water hung parallel from a scrawny metal arm as tall as Lanie, if she stood on tiptoes. She followed the red and clear tubes that connected the bottoms of each bag to her body. It was plasma running to the bend in her elbow, and something thicker than water and slightly yellowish running to the back of her opposite hand. Tape over cotton balls held them in place. A plastic finger-puppet covered her index finger, which fed another wire to a monitor with out-of-focus and ever-changing numbers and zigzags. If she concentrated on the number beneath the heart long enough, she could make it go up or down by at least ten.

Gauze as thick as hands covered her bad arm from wrist to elbow where the man in the backseat of the Buick had slashed with the knife. More covered her chest—she felt the tape against her skin at least—although a blue paper shirt hid other places where it hurt. Small bowtie bandages covered most of her exposed skin. Lanie imagined a cloud of white butterflies fluttering in from the window that morning in the hospital room (definitely a hospital room by the smell of it) to rest their wings on her body. From the corner of her eyes, she could see edges of similar bandages on her face, perhaps covering her entire head. Her pulse pressed through her neck, and what felt like cracks in her skull. The heart rate number on the monitor matched the hot throbs seconds later, or perhaps seconds before.

A brace with pins held her left leg in place; tape and more gauze covered her right. And the fluorescent light covered her bruises and exposed cuts with purple shadow.

The pain was everywhere, but her head hurt the most, and then her stomach. Her entire right arm didn't hurt at all because it was numb, like her new robotic-looking leg. Lanie peeled back the largest bandage on her arm to discover someone had sewn the biggest pieces of her arm with black crisscrosses of thread.

All the king's horses and all the king's men …

"You should leave that alone," said a man. "Or they'll never be able to put you back together again."

He appeared like the others, faceless, but only because he sat in the chair nearest to what looked to be the way out—signified by the soft red glow of an EXIT sign. Everything within arm's distance was fuzzy; everything farther than the clock was unrecognizable, made of shapeless paint-swirls of color.

If only Lanie could paint the room how she wanted to imagine it.

Her hand, the one that had gone through the driver's face, was shattered, she knew, beneath the splints and tape and white bandages that clumped the broken fingers together like a torch ready to be lit. She could light it and not feel a thing.

"Leave what alone?" Lanie asked. It would be rude to

let the man wait any longer for her answer, but when her voice scratched out those words, she wished she had kept them inside longer because they hurt.

Lanie didn't sound like Lanie; she sounded like a little boy with a sore throat.

"Alone …" she repeated, to hear the voice again.

"The stitches," said the man. "You picked at them in your sleep, and you're picking at them now. Any longer and you'll pull them out and bleed to death."

"Who are you and why are you in my room?"

"My name is Asche, and you're not in your room; you're in a hospital."

"Ash?"

"Spelled differently. Do you remember what happened?"

"Why is it so hard to talk?"

"I overheard the nurse say one of your lungs was punctured when she went over your chart, as well as your neck. And both your collar bones are busted. You lost a lot of blood. You're lucky to be breathing on your own, let alone to have lived after what you went through."

"It's the right one."

"Right one?"

"Feels like I swallowed a balloon and it overinflated in my chest. You know how the rubber gets when you blow it up and then let the air out? A few times and the balloon gets thin. But I don't feel lucky, I feel tired."

"It's okay to sleep. I'll watch over you."

She was about to ask again who he was, who he really was, but the man faded with the rest of the hospital room and she fell asleep for what felt like a moment.

2001 (28)

"I'm tired," said the boy at her side.

"A few more blocks," she said, holding his hand tightly. Someone had taken Nicole's daughter home; somehow Lanie had ended up with the boy.

She also held a girl who couldn't have weighed more than twenty pounds. She had found her near a park bench, arms at her side, eyes wide and wet and with dry-muddy streaks down her cheeks. She wasn't crying when Lanie found her; she was long past crying. Lanie and the boy had stayed with her until staying was no longer an option.

She led them away.

The lost looked for loved ones and answers, coughing The City from their lungs. Gray clothes and gray skin camouflaged against a gray backdrop

Like everyone else, they were completely lost in the chaos, so she listened for sirens to fade, always heading the opposite direction of the fire trucks and ambulances and police cruisers.

The dead slept in the streets where the smoke was strongest. Thousands of them. Those who worked in The City's biggest teeth were gone. All of them, including Nicole.

Lanie had averted the boy's eyes, turning him away after seeing the first of the blackbirds cartwheeling through the air, some of them cartwheeling together, but she was unable to look away, only able to turn away when the first building sank into the ground, burying the people who chose to stay inside. Nic was gone and she could no longer—

1990 (17)

"Drop with me."

"Nic, I've got a chemistry final at—"

"Fuck chemistry," she said. "Besides, this *is* chemistry."

Lanie took the Visine bottle from her and thought of unscrewing the lid and dumping the *D5* down the kitchen sink. But that would be five hundred down the drain and only half of that had been hers. Dropping would last an hour, tops, with most of the psychotropic effects wearing off before the first morning bell.

"Come on. Drop with me. *Please.*"

Lanie leaned back and squeezed a drop into each eye.

The rush was instant.

Her best friend smiled a deteriorating bloody smile that slowly elongated, as if her mouth had been sheared open to give her a wide, skeletal grin. Skin melted from her face as freely as hot candle wax. The world turned black and white, swirling with oleaginous color.

Lanie felt the bottle leaving her hands as Nic took it from her in the slowest of motions. Skin, so soft and delicate as fingers brushed against her own. Upon blinking, Nic was beautiful and glowed radiant turquoise.

Her own skin swam in the palest of yellows.

Tears welled as Lanie blinked through hallucinations.

1988 (15)

He was still there when her eyes opened: Ash, but spelled differently. The clock on the wall was too blurry to read, but she thought the smaller hand pointed to six … still. She had slept for twelve hours, or maybe none—the curtains were drawn shut—yet he was still in the chair by the door without a book or a magazine or anything else to keep him busy.

"How's the balloon in your chest?" he said.

Lanie took a deep breath to see how much would inflate.

"Thin," she said. Her voice sounded like a sick boy's.

"I saw the accident, which is why I'm here."

She could see him now, better than before, at least, although he remained fuzzy and faceless, like the man in the car.

"What did you see?"

What, really, did *she* see?

"You were riding your bike on the sidewalk and they struck you."

The way this ash man said *they* was accusatory.

"Or, something else," he said.

That meant he knew about the man in the backseat. He could very well *be* the man from the backseat. He could have followed her to the hospital, or had perhaps taken her there, and was now patiently waiting for the right opportunity to finish what he had failed to do after *they* had mowed her down with the gray Buick.

[The sound of the undercarriage of the car grating the curb …]

Why was the passenger seat empty?

[The sound of bicycle hitting bumper …]

They had meant to hit her. The passenger seat was empty, for *her*, in case she'd gone through the windshield instead of bouncing off, in case she didn't get pulled underneath like the bike, in case she didn't vault off the metal hood and tumble over.

[The sound of breaking glass …]

Neither expected the driver to die, or for Lanie to end up in the backseat of the Buick. The man in the backseat had been in shock, like Lanie, with blood—not his—splattered across his face. These men, they'd expected the car to kill her.

The shocked man sticking her with his pocketknife and slashing at her wrists, he was afraid; he had meant to kill her, but was too scared to do it properly.

To kill something, some*one*, you really had to have it in you.

"So you saw what happened?"

[The sound of fist through face …]

"I did," the man said. "Actually, I may have seen two things, simultaneously, but I'm not sure I believe them both. I saw a gray Buick swerve and jounce onto the curb, striking you; yet at the same time, I saw your bike veer toward the street, handlebar jerking to the left just before the accident. What I want to believe is that your handlebar jerking to the left was an involuntary movement, that you hit a divot in the concrete; what I don't want to believe is that it was voluntary. Did you want to die?"

"I can't remember. Maybe. I don't know."

"Have you ever thought of that?"

"Everyone's thought of that. Who are you, anyway?"

"I'm a guy who saw something bad happen, a guy who was interviewed by the police to report to them what I saw, from my point of view."

"What was your point of view?"

It hurt so much to talk, to simply keep her eyes open. Something rested in his lap: a knife, or a paperback novel, on its side—her eyes offered a dark knife-shaped / book-shaped blur and nothing more.

Perhaps his point of view was the backseat of the Buick.

"Are you here to kill me?" said the scratchy boy voice.

Lanie's head pounded. The room had become tipsy. The white walls and tile floor appeared to vibrate because of the twitching of her left eye, the fluorescents above her bed humming abnormally loud. Everything white in the room darkened.

The man without a face adjusted in his seat and for a moment a wide shadow stretched out to either side of him, like black feathery wings.

"You're going to have some nasty scars," he said.

Lanie blinked heavily and he was gone.

1989 (16)

Standing in front of a full-length mirror, she removed her blouse, kicked her Lucky jeans to the floor, pushed the mass of fallen clothes with bare toes. Her fingers traced the white railroad tracks, one by one. The scars, so many of them, held her together for the moment. Lanie tilted her head back and admired the thick lines on her neck, along with those across her chest and her arms, as well as the markings left behind on her reconstructed leg and hand.

From the left side of her forehead—right in the mirror—to her lower lip, another scar ran across her face, directly over her eye. The right eye in her reflection—left in reality—closed and the world became clear. Upon opening, the world was covered in a moderate haze, due to her right eye dominance; closing that dominant eye, the world was as scratched as her cornea, as if viewed through water. She preferred the haze, however, because her once immaculate body was, as Nic would put it, fucked.

She dripped drops from the Visine bottle into her eyes, one by one.

The rush was instant.

Her throat opened in another moment, and in another, her wrist. White scars turned red, but they were only scars: memories of hurt. In the reflection, memories dripped onto the carpet and pooled at her feet as her body opened, like some morbid jigsaw puzzle of flesh starting to peel away at the edges. A thick scar covered her chest from armpit to armpit, although that wound in particular was not a result of the accident.

She blinked in the drug, and the memories were gone. So were the scars.

Sixteen years old and not a blemish.

Part of her knew the mirror was a liar; part of her liked knowing the mirror sometimes lied. "You don't have to lie to make friends," someone told her once. Sometimes that was the lie.

Lanie's reflected skin held that innocent, teenage softness she so often admired of her friends, and those pretending to be her friends, and those who had unfriended her following the accident. She had quickly turned from popular to unpopular over the course of the school year. She had become damaged, a person with whom others were afraid to be seen.

Gone now were the injuries.

Gone now were the disfigurements.

Gone now were the mutilations.

The reflection revealed a beautiful sixteen-year-old girl, a sophomore in high school ready to turn junior, and she was just fine with that. Although unable to remember much from her life before the accident, Lanie imagined this was what she looked like before—

She blinked and the ugliness returned.

She blinked, letting the drug do its magic.

1990 (17)

"Drop with me again," Nic said through swirls of color.

Lanie swung by her knees from the lowest pull-up bar with Nicole at her side. The wet tips of their ponytails dangled to brushstroke the flowers below. Together, upside-down, they painted the world in a different image.

They dropped single drops of *D5* into each of their eyes and welcomed the rush—

2001 (28)

—of emergency vehicles and people on foot littered the streets of The City. Lanie held onto the nameless girl. Lanie had asked the girl her name, but the girl, no heavier than a bag of groceries, simply stared not at her, but through her. The boy, holding Lanie's hand as tightly as she held onto his, followed along, distracted. His hair, once dirty brown, had become gray from dead buildings and dead—

"Do you remember your address?" she had asked.

She wondered about Nicole's daughter, and whether or not she made it home.

"Yes."

"What is it? We should take you there. Maybe your parents are looking for you at home since, well, since the bus can't take you."

She wasn't even sure he was supposed to ride the school bus, or *any* bus, for that matter. The poor kid was in shock and could barely remember his own name—which was James Michael Thompson, he had told her after thinking hard—let alone remember whether or not he had gotten on the bus after school had let out early, or if he was supposed to wait for a ride, or if his parents were planning to pick him up. When she found him, James had ventured aimlessly for who-knows how long through the cloud that had enveloped The City's heart.

"Apartment two."

"Apartment two?"

"Uh huh."

"Is that all you remember of the address? Do you remember the street name and number, or which borough, even?"

"Just apartment two," the boy said. "We live in apartment two."

"How about a phone number?"

The boy nodded ardently.

Lanie let go of his hand, long enough to check her cellphone for a signal, knowing she'd either have zero bars or zero chance of connecting a call. A dozen tries and no luck, but what hurt could one more call …? She managed to retrieve it from her pocket, despite the dusty potato sack girl in her arms. And her heart sank. She turned to the boy, but he was gone. Footprints of all sizes cratered the sidewalk like the remnants of a hundred dancers. She looked for James-sized prints on the ground before the wind had the chance to hide them forever.

"James?"

A slumped woman bumped against her shoulder, apologized without looking, and kept walking, head down. A police officer on a bike swerved around them and was gone before Lanie thought to call out to him for help. Sirens mocked her cries. Through the ash-storm, visibility teased twenty feet in any direction and then turned into an endless wall of dust and smoke and death and everything else that floated in the air.

How could she have lost him so easily? He couldn't have gone far, only a few steps. She had promised to take him home, had pinky-sworn to help find his family. Yet the smallest of distractions and he was … he was gone, like so many other children that morning. So many little feet, all dancing to a waltz—

> One two three:
> > We can dance
> > > Hand in hand
> > > > Feet on feet

> One two three:
> > Grab on tight
> > > Float with me
> > > > To the sky

One two three:
   Lend your ear
      To my lips
         Smile with me

She imagined the spirits of thousands, swirling to the heavens, one step at a time, perhaps keeping step to the whisper dance—

One two three:
     Spin you round
        Close your eyes
          Trust in me

One two three:
   You will see
      Where we go
         When we both

One two three …

She imagined the boy dancing, his tiny gray-powdered Skechers resting upon the feet of an older dead man or older dead woman, smaller hands held between larger hands. Nearly invisible, they'd dance and swirl and dance and swirl, up and up and up and up …

"James Michael Thompson?"

Hand in hand, feet on feet—

The woman who had bumped into her had a child at her side, and the child hesitated at being pulled in that direction at the sound of Lanie's cracked voice. Another step and the ash-fall haze swallowed them both, as easily as a few of The City's teeth had swallowed buildings whole.

1983 (10)

196 was the address of the old Hopkins House before it burned to nothing but a scorched skeletal frame and had to be rebuilt to the new Hopkins House. The numbers dangled before falling to the ground. How did the fire start, they asked, those in the dressy clothes and uniforms, and was it an accident, because they could tell if it wasn't an accident and had ways of knowing after investigations if lighters or matches or children were to blame, they said, most of it not even sounding like questions, but more like rambling run-on sentences. So many anxious fingers looked for places to point, so many questions—

"What time is it?"

[a breath / a puff]

without inflections as the other boys and girls and caregivers, all full from having just eaten a late supper, crowded around the giant oak in front of what used to be the original Hopkins House before it fell. A boy with choppy hair the color and oiliness of tar picked up his toy airplane, a matte black SR-71 jet, which matched Lanie's own charred hair, and tried to bend back the wings since it was trampled, also, much like her hair. A nurse dabbed a rag with ointment against Lanie's scalp, ever so gently, as the previously screaming children were consoled to mere whimpers by adults who no longer needed to herd them around; they were all so tired and scared, auras no longer billowing from bodies, but wafting off them in the night air. Broken glass from shattered windows speckled the grass. Sirens no longer sang. The book of matches in Lanie's pocket—

At least seven o'clock.

"What time is it?"

[a breath / a puff]

tied her to everything that had happened. She would need to hide the book somewhere, or better yet *discard*—a word she thought her father might've used to say—the matches down the sewer drain, perhaps, "where shit goes when you no longer have it in you"—was that her father, too?—but the memories, they would … they would always be there, or they should be there at least … but yet they wouldn't, they *weren't* there, because the damn memories were only fragments, or perhaps *figments* of—

At least eight o'clock.

"What time is it?"

[a breath / a puff]

dreaming. So much dreaming.

At least nine o'clock.

1988 (15)

"You're having a nightmare," the blurry man said, shaking her arm.

"I was?"

"You were. You called out a name: Nicole. And your

nonbandaged arm was flapping, as if you were trying to fly, and you called out her name."

"*This* isn't the nightmare?" Lanie said, and looked around the hospital room. The lights were dim, the walls no longer white, but whitish blue. The clock on the wall told her it was a few minutes after nine.

"I watched her jump. She was much older, like you. Not old, but older, you know? An adult. And I watched her jump."

"And you were counting, over and over again."

"I don't remember. It's gone now."

"How's the balloon in your chest?"

"Still there. Is it early nine o'clock, or late nine o'clock?"

"Late."

"And you've been here the whole time?"

The man, Ash—but spelled differently, stepped back and sat in the chair by the door where she had first noticed him. She thought he nodded, but if so, it had been subtle. The black wings she thought she had seen earlier were as gone as her dream.

A woman in scrubs joined them. She cradled a clip-board in one arm and pointed at the attached papers with a pen. She flicked one of the IV bags.

"You're awake," she said, as if surprised.

"I think so."

"Good. Let's get those bandages changed. Are the drugs working for you? We've been giving you the good stuff, so hopefully the pain's minimal."

"Can you see him, too?" Lanie asked, pointed her not-so-damaged hand at Ash—but spelled differently.

2001 (28)

The boy had disappeared in a matter of seconds, taken as easily as her childhood. How old was he? Nine, eight, seven? She was never good at estimating the ages of children, mostly because her childhood had been taken, had become a blur—

1982 (9)

Nothing there.

1981 (8)

Nothing there.

1980 (7)

Nothing there.

2001 (28)

Lanie cradled the rag doll girl and pursued the boy—James Michael Thompson; she had learned his name and would always remember it. The girl, however, was unable to say her name. Lanie wiped the ash from around her eyes, which stared past Lanie, to the sky.

"We'll find him," she told the girl, patting her back.

Newer, smaller footprints pointed toward the path of the lady who had bumped into her. A small set of tracks next to a larger set of tracks. The woman had held onto the arm of a boy as well, perhaps James, perhaps unaware she had even acquired a child. Lanie ran in that direction, holding the girl close to her chest.

"Wait," she called out. "Wait!"

In a few strides, the woman and the boy at her side came into being once again, as if materializing from nothing. The boy wore a New York Yankees hat, or perhaps the Mets, the NY letters buried in The City dust. Had he worn a hat? Why couldn't she remember something as simple as that?

"James," she said, bending down and pulling at his free hand, and he spun around, which spun the lady around holding onto his other hand, but the boy wasn't James, although he looked as scared as any other child she had seen that morning.

She expected the woman to berate her, but she smiled an unfriendly smile, tugged the boys arm, and continued dragging him onward. Perhaps the boy wasn't hers, but one she had acquired, one she wouldn't lose, no matter what.

"Have you seen a boy?" Lanie asked. "By himself?"

"If I saw a boy by himself," the woman said, walking away, "I would make sure he wasn't by himself." And then she and the boy in the hat were absorbed by the haze.

This left her two directions to search: perpendiculars to the way she had come and the way she was going. She had to find the boy, couldn't leave him alone … One direction led across the street through a labyrinth of gridlocked cars; the other led to an alley.

"Hold on," she told the girl in her arms.

Lanie ran toward the alley until she noticed an absence of footprints in the ash. The alley was empty and appeared to end in chainlink fence. She turned around and stopped at the curb and looked both directions, despite the dead street. Although most vehicles were abandoned, and those occupied weren't going anywhere, their windows rolled up to protect those inside from the powdery air, she looked both directions. She was protecting the child, Lanie realized; otherwise, she would have charged through the street, slaloming around the cars parked and covered in the ash snow.

The boy was shorter than the tops of most hoods, so she crawled onto the hood of a once-yellow taxi—nestling the girl—and rose. Her feet slid in the slag-like material, but felt stable, so she climbed higher, stepping on the wipers for leverage, onto the roof. She planted her feet around the still-glowing TAXI roof light, and called out his name with a cupped mouth.

"James!" she called out again, and then she found him, hunkered next to the rear wheel of a bread truck, arms wrapped around his knees, head tucked into the gap such a position created.

He lifted his head and turned to her voice.

The third time she shouted his name he saw her, and got to his feet.

"Stay there," she said. "I'll come to you."

He understood and told her so by nodding.

She slipped, landing on her ass, and it made her laugh as she cuddled the girl tighter. Lanie swiveled, let her body slide down the windshield, and then down the hood until her feet made contact with the asphalt. She told the girl everything would be all right, that she'd somehow find their parents and help them home.

James brightened when Lanie edged around back-to-back black MINI Coopers. She quickstepped to him, kneeled to his level, and brushed hair from his eyes.

"You okay, buddy?"

He smiled. "The white building next to the park with the swings. Apartment two. But I don't know the address."

"Next to the swings, is there a big broken fountain?"

"A fairy fountain?"

Lanie took his hand.

"Let's take you home."

Nineteen blocks and they were at the park. Lanie remembered swinging upside-down from the middle swing as a child, and as a teenager, and later, many times, as an adult, her hair dangling to the ground as she watched teeth of The City bite the sky.

What were the odds the boy lived next door?

The boy's mother ran down the steps, across the yard.

"James? Oh, thank God!" she said, crying and patting his hair and face, as if checking to see if he were real. An aura-like puff of The City's dust floated around him. "I left work and came home because the schools said they were letting everyone out and sending kids home." She kissed him on his dirty cheek, as well as his forehead, leaving behind gray lip prints. "James, it's really you. I tried calling the school a hundred times but the lines are busy or down or I don't know but you're home. You're really home."

Lanie began to back away, to head toward Hopkins House, which wasn't far away. Perhaps there, they could call around, or attempt to call around, depending on service. The little nameless girl in her arms also had a home. Perhaps those at Hopkins House could take her in until the girl's shock wore off—her own shock as well—enough to get more information out of her: a name, where her parents worked, anything that could help.

"Thank you," the mother said, with the most serious look on her face Lanie had ever seen. "Thank you," she said again and cried. This woman exuded such an indescribable push of emotion. In a much shakier voice, a throat coated with sand, the woman—Mrs. Thompson—said, "Is she yours?"

Lanie rocked the child, unsure when she had started the motion. She had had a doll once, she could remember, but couldn't remember much more than that. She imagined herself as a child, perhaps James' age, holding onto a doll just like this, rocking the small form in her arms like mothers were supposed to do.

"Someone else's," she said, combing fingers through the girl's hair. "I'm not sure who she belongs to."

The woman stepped forward and touched the child.

"I'm so—" the mother said, putting a hand to her mouth. "I'm so sorry." The emotion or energy or whatever Lanie had felt emanating from the woman died, and she found the woman crying different kinds of tears. "Where did you find her body?"

Lanie stopped rocking and looked down to the still child, her own shock instantly worn away by the question, and then she remembered where and when and how she had found the child and it all came rushing—

1988 (15)

Drugs, whatever new warmth the nurse had given her, coursed through her body, eliminating the pain to which her body had tried to adapt. The rush was instant.

"What if he comes back?" Lanie asked. "The man who did this?"

"I'll make sure that doesn't happen," said Asche.

Lanie imagined his name spelled that way, different from the stuff that fell around her and the other girls at the first Hopkins House the night it burned. Was that a memory? She vaguely remembered a charred, skeletal frame—of a building, of a body?—and then it was gone.

Asche could very well be the man who did this to her. But so what? So what if he finished the job and helped her die? Was he watching her to make sure she couldn't remember who he was or what he looked like? Was he waiting around to see if she could do just that after all the king's horses and all the king's men tried to put Lanie back together again?

Shadows behind her protector—as Lanie liked to think of him—resembled black wings once again, but it was merely moonlight permeating through the mini blinds of the window.

"I'm here to make sure you're safe."

1983 (10)

"You'll be safe here," said the caregiver. The sun had gone down hours ago, much past the time at which she normally found herself under the covers. "Lots of girls—"

At least ten o'clock.

"What time is it?"

[a breath / a puff]

"—your age are here, Lanie, some younger, even. There's a girl half your age staying here as well."

The building stood three stories high and seemed to take up most of the block. Worn wooden siding climbed the exterior walls; once probably white, transformed by weather over time to a dirty off-white. Seven steps led to the entryway where two yellowish lights hung from a ceiling surrounded by gray plaster of Paris molds. The sign above the door read HOPKINS—

At least eleven o'clock.

"What time is it?"

[a breath / a puff]

—HOUSE in a newer coat of paint, the letters white against slate gray, vibrant compared to the rest of the building. Lanie swallowed the lump in her throat and ascended the steps, which each required two of her own steps. This would be her new home—

At least twelve o'clock.

"What time is it?"

[a breath / a puff]

for as long as they would have her, for as long as she needed to stay to get *better*, as her examiner put it— however long that may be, or perhaps for as long as state law required. Could she get better? Was anything wrong with her?

Her world flipped upside-down.

1990 (17)

Lanie swung by her knees from a pull-up bar in the park, her ponytail dangling to brushstroke the ground where, some-day, living people would bury no-longer-living people. The City's two tallest teeth protruded from the ground / sky, filled with thousands upon thousands of people.

Ash fluttered down, or perhaps up, to the gray blanket covering a ground that had become her sky. It was only snow, but Lanie always thought snow looked like ash.

One day they will dig deep holes and build buildings like these, she mused, downward instead of upward, into the ground, not above it, to bury all the people in the world when they die: skyscraper tombs to take care of overpopulation and death.

1993 (20)

Lanie hesitated over the Visine bottle.

2003 (30)

Pull up if I pull up, she mused, and righted herself on the pull-up bar.

The fairy fountain next to her spurted. As far as she could remember, it had never worked before, but suddenly sprung to life and spit at the air, the water rising into the sky and falling to the ground. She thought of Nicole and imagined her body cartwheeling in reverse, un-falling. She thought of Nicole's child, wondering if she had ever made it home. She thought of the boy named James. She thought of the unnamed girl. She tried to remember her past.

Lanie grabbed one of the dandelion clocks at her feet, brought the white puff to her lips and took a deep breath.

What time is it? she wondered.

Whisper Dance

One two three

We can dance
Hand in hand
Feet on feet

One two three

Grab on tight
Float with me
To the sky

One two three

Lend your ear
To my lips
Smile with me

One two three

Spin you round
Close your eyes
Trust in me

One two three

You will see
Where we go
When we both

One two three …

About the Author

Michael Bailey is a multi-award-winning author, editor and publisher, and the recipient of over two dozen literary accolades, including the Bram Stoker Award, Benjamin Franklin Award, Eric Hoffer Book Award, Independent Publisher Book Award, the Indie Book Award, the International Book Award, and others. His novels include *Palindrome Hannah*, *Phoenix Rose* and *Psychotropic Dragon*, and he has published two short story and poetry collections, *Scales and Petals*, and *Inkblots and Blood Spots* (illustrated by Daniele Serra, with an introduction by Douglas E. Winter).

He is also the founder of the small press Written Backwards, where he has created psychological horror anthologies such as *Pellucid Lunacy*, *The Library of the Dead*, four volumes of *Chiral Mad* (the fourth co-edited by Lucy A. Snyder), and a few dark science fiction anthologies such as *Qualia Nous* and *You, Human*. He also served as the co-editor of both *Adam's Ladder* and *Prisms* (with Darren Speegle). Most recent publications include *Oversight*, a collection of novelettes including *Darkroom* and *SAD Face*, and the standalone novelette *Our Children, Our Teachers*. He lives in forever-burning California.

You can follow him on social media at twitter.com/nettirw, facebook.com/nettirw, or online at www.nettirw.com.

www.ingramcontent.com/pod-product-compliance
Lightning Source LLC
Chambersburg PA
CBHW050231110726
47898CB00007B/2112